Nightmare at the Book Fair

ALSO BY DAN GUTMAN

Nightmare at the Book Fair

AT THE
BOOK FAIR

AUTHOR OF
DAN GUTMAN
The
HOMEWORK · MACHINE

SIMON & SCHUSTER BOOKS FOR YOUNG READERS

New York   London   Toronto   Sydney

SIMON & SCHUSTER BOOKS FOR YOUNG READERS
An imprint of Simon & Schuster Children's Publishing Division
1230 Avenue of the Americas, New York, New York 10020
This book is a work of fiction. Any references to historical events, real people, or real locales are used fictitiously. Other names, characters, places, and incidents are products of the author's imagination, and any resemblance to actual events or locales or persons, living or dead, is entirely coincidental.
Copyright © 2008 by Dan Gutman
All rights reserved, including the right of reproduction in whole or in part in any form.
SIMON & SCHUSTER BOOKS FOR YOUNG READERS is a trademark of Simon & Schuster, Inc.
For information about special discounts for bulk purchases, please contact
Simon & Schuster Special Sales at 1-866-506-1949 or business@simonandschuster.com.
The Simon & Schuster Speakers Bureau can bring authors to your live event. For more information or to book an event, contact the Simon & Schuster Speakers Bureau at 1-866-248-3049 or visit our website at www.simonspeakers.com.
Also available in a Simon & Schuster Books for Young Readers hardcover edition.
Book design by Tom Daly
The text for this book is set in Aldine 401 BT.
Manufactured in the United States of America • 0510 OFF
First Simon & Schuster Books for Young Readers paperback edition June 2010
10 9 8 7 6 5 4 3 2 1
The Library of Congress has cataloged the hardcover edition as follows:
Gutman, Dan
Nightmare at the book fair/Dan Gutman
p. cm
Summary: When fifth-grader Trip Dinkleman, who does not like to read very much, is hit on the head by a heavy box and becomes a character in a series of different books—from a sports story to a science fiction novel to an adventure tale—his view of reading is changed forever.
ISBN 978-1-4169-2438-8 (hc)
[1.Books and reading—Fiction] I. Title II. Nightmare at the book fair.
PZ7.G9846Ni 2008
[Fic]—dc22
2007039243
ISBN 978-1-4169-2439-5 (pbk)
ISBN 978-1-4165-7948-9 (eBook)

To all the PTA moms and dads
who donate their time and energy
to making book fairs happen at their school

Contents

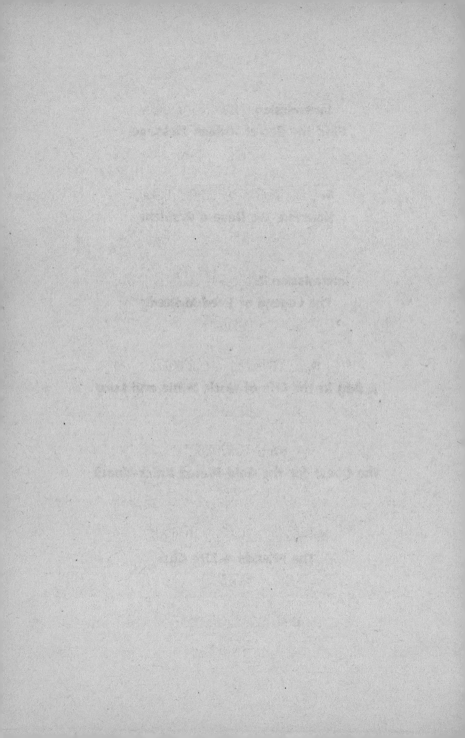

Chapter 1

The Book Fair

"Hey Dinkleman!"

I turned around. Lionel Jordan slammed his locker shut and slung his backpack over his shoulder. The three o'clock bell had just rung and the hallway was filling up with kids. Lionel and I have been best friends since I don't know when.

"You tryin' out for lacrosse, Dink?" Lionel asked.

"No doubt," I told him. "I'll meet you over at the field."

In most towns, middle school starts in sixth grade. But they had some overcrowding problem in the elementary schools, so they had to put the fifth grade into the middle school in our town. That meant we got lockers, and we didn't have to sit in one room staring at the same teacher all day. It also meant we could go out for sports for the first time. I thought about trying out for football, because I'm pretty big for my age. But I'm not very good. Me and Lionel decided we'd have the best chance of making the lacrosse team because all their best players moved up to high school this year.

"I hope you make the team, Trip," my social studies teacher, Mrs. Babcock, said as she walked by my locker. "Don't forget to study for the quiz tomorrow."

"Oh, I'll know everything about the three branches of government, Mrs. Babcock," I promised.

The media center is right around the corner from my locker. There was a big sign on the wall— THIS WAY TO THE BOOK FAIR!

Ugh. I make it a point not to set foot in the media center if I can help it. I don't like to read.

Never did. I mean, I read okay, I guess. I read when I have to. It's just kind of boring to sit there looking at words on a page. I'd rather run around.

One time the media specialist, Miss Durkin, told me that if I like sports so much, I would probably enjoy reading sports books. But why read about kids running around playing sports when I can be running around playing sports myself?

"Excuse me, is your name Trip Dinkleman?"

It was Mrs. Pontoon, president of the PTA. She was standing outside the media center. I guess she knew my name because her daughter Lauren is in a few of my classes.

"Yes?"

"We need a big strong boy to help us move some crates," Mrs. Pontoon said. "Can you help us out?"

"I'm kind of on my way to lacrosse tryouts," I told her.

"Oh, this will only take a few minutes."

Snagged! I followed her into the media center. Mrs. Pontoon talks really fast.

"The PTA wants to buy the school one of those super high-tech whiteboards, you know, the kind that hook up to a computer and you can print things out?" Mrs. Pontoon said, barely stopping to take a breath. "But they're very expensive so we had to raise the money, and my original plan was to hold a fund raiser where we'd have the students sell gift wrapping paper, but Principal Miller didn't like the idea of kids knocking on strangers' doors so he said we could have a book fair instead and we need some help because Mr. Dunn the custodian told me he had to mop the cafeteria so it will dry in time for the chorus to come in so it's very nice of you to help. . . ."

Mrs. Pontoon is one of those ladies who never stops talking. My mom says that if you asked Mrs. Pontoon what time it is, she would tell you how to build a clock.

The book fair wasn't set up yet in the media

center. They had these giant crates—taller than me—scattered around. There must have been ten of them. Mrs. Pontoon told me that all the books for the book fair were in the crates. She needed help opening them and sliding them into a line along the wall. I pushed against one of the crates. It was really heavy. This was going to be a big job.

If I had finished at my locker a few seconds earlier, it occurred to me, I would be at lacrosse tryouts instead of helping set up the book fair.

Miss Durkin came over with a plate full of cookies. I have a total sweet tooth, and I pounced on it.

"Since you're nice enough to help, Trip, the least I can do is offer you a treat."

I feel sorry for Miss Durkin. She's always really busy because she's also the media specialist at my old elementary school. She works there three days a week and comes to our school for two days. And she doesn't even have an assistant. She always seems stressed out.

I opened the latch on one of the big crates and pushed the two sides apart. When the crate was opened up, it was like a big set of bookshelves. It was filled with picture books for little kids. The books were all lined up and organized, ready for kids to buy them. Maybe it wouldn't take too long after all.

I struggled to push open the next crate, which was even heavier. When I finally got it open, I could see why it was so heavy. It was filled with dictionaries and encyclopedias. Ugh. Who would want to buy one of *them*?

The crate was too heavy to slide. I had to rock it back and forth to get it to move across the floor. That's what I was doing when, suddenly, I don't know what happened, I guess I rocked it too much or, I don't know, but some of those fat ones on the top shelf must have leaned or something, and the next thing I knew the whole shelfful of them was coming down, and I tried to get my hands up, but . . .

Bam! Oh, my head!

Chapter 2

Horror

Sugar Shock

Oh, my head!

When I opened my eyes, a reflection in a mirror was staring at me. I shrank back in terror. My face was bent and distorted into a tortured, grotesque mask of disfigurement! Somehow, sometime, somewhere, I had been turned into a horrible, disgusting, hideous-looking monster!

But no.

As it turned out, the reflection was in a curvy fun-house mirror, the kind you see at carnivals and science museums. When I squatted down a few inches, the mirror compressed my body into a funny-looking Humpty Dumpty shape. When I stood on my tiptoes, it appeared that my head had separated from the rest of my body and was floating a few inches above it.

Whew! What a relief!

"Hey kid," mumbled a female voice behind me. "You want a free ticket to the haunted house?"

I turned around to see a punky-looking teenage girl, with short black hair and a tattoo of a tiger on her neck. There were scars on her face, as if she had been in an accident and needed a lot of stitches. She held out a ticket for me.

"I've already been inside," she added.

"Is it scary?" I asked.

"Dude," she replied, "this is the scariest haunted house you'll ever visit."

I couldn't tell if she was being sarcastic or not.

Looking over her shoulder, I could see that I was standing on a boardwalk, one of those honky-tonk strips down the shore crammed with T-shirt shops, saltwater taffy vendors, and cheesy carnival rides. I could feel the breeze, smell the ocean. Right next to the haunted house was a booth with a college kid trying to talk people into shooting a basketball at a hoop to win stuffed animals. Clearly, it was a rip-off. The rim was hardly any bigger than the ball.

On the other side of the haunted house was a booth selling funnel cake. Ummm. Good smell. I could almost taste it.

What am I doing here? What happened to the book fair? Is this a dream? Is this heaven? Am I in a coma? Is this what it feels like to be unconscious? Or am I on some dumb reality TV show?

I didn't know. And you know what? I didn't care, either. Whatever it was, I decided, I was going to enjoy it.

"Sure, yeah, why not?" I said, taking the ticket. The girl snickered and walked away.

Haunted house. Yeah, right! I've been to dozens of these places. They're always the same. Bored actors in cheap zombie costumes jump out at you from behind corners and scream. Eyes on portraits follow you as you walk by. Fake bats. Disembodied limbs nailed to the walls. Weak-looking holographic ghosts. Spooky voices and howling wolves come out of cheap speakers. They're always lame.

I slipped the ticket into a slot, which made the gate in front of me swing open. It also made another gate come down behind me. I turned around and pushed against that one. It wouldn't budge. There was no way to go backward.

Hmmm.

I thought about climbing over the fence and getting out of there. But then I saw the small sign: DO NOT TOUCH! 50,000 VOLTS. Maybe it was just a prop, another part of the "terrifying" experience. But maybe it was real. Maybe if I touched it, 50,000 volts would shoot through my body. It wasn't a chance I was willing to take.

The steps creaked eerily as I climbed them. Nice effect. It didn't even sound computer generated. The front door opened before I could put my hand on the doorknob and closed behind me as soon as I went inside.

I wasn't scared. Not yet.

"Hello?" I called out, as I walked down the hallway. "Anybody home?"

Nobody was around. The hallway was lit by dim lightbulbs so I could hardly see anything at all. The wallpaper was old and faded. Not bad. They had done a pretty good job on the place. It really looked like an old house.

You couldn't hear the sounds of the boardwalk in the distance. There was no carnival music playing, no happy shrieks from the kids on the roller coaster. Good soundproofing. Impressive.

Then I heard something like a series of clicks on the wood floor. A moment later, a black cat jumped out right in front of me, hissing and spit-ting. It wasn't some fake animatronic cat. This was a *real* cat. How did they get that cat to perform on command? My cat at home won't do *anything*. Just then, a strobe light flashed and I looked into the cat's eyes.

The cat had the face of a *dog*!

I screamed as I backed up against the wall behind me. Okay, *now* I was scared. More than scared. They had scared the crap out of me.

This was a big mistake on my part, I realized. What had I gotten myself into? I never should have taken the ticket from that girl. Now I had to find my way out of the place.

All the doors on the first floor were locked. I ran upstairs, searching desperately for a red exit sign. Aren't they required by law to have them in places like this? What if there's a fire? No time to worry about that now.

There was a kitchen on the second floor with a

round table in the middle of it. And in the middle of the table was a round plate. And in the middle of the round plate was one of the few things in the world that I truly loved.

A funnel cake.

Have you ever had funnel cake? If you've never had it, you're missing one of the great joys of life. One of the main reasons we were put on this earth. Without funnel cake, life would hardly be worth living.

A funnel cake doesn't look like a funnel. It's more like a big waffle with powdered sugar sprinkled on top. I'll tell you, if you put powdered sugar on *anything*, it will taste good. They should put powdered sugar on broccoli and asparagus and other stuff that kids don't want to eat. But when you put powdered sugar on something that is already incredible tasting to begin with, you're about to eat perfection.

I looked at the funnel cake. It was just sitting there. It looked so good. I wanted to get out of there, but I wanted the funnel cake too. I broke off a little piece and popped it into my mouth. Oh, man! I couldn't stop myself. I grabbed the thing and stuffed the rest of it into my mouth. Never in my life had I tasted a funnel cake as good as this one.

"What a nice face you have," spoke a low voice from the shadowy corner of the room.

"Ahhhhh!"

The guy took a step forward into the dim light. I could see he was wearing a checked bathrobe and slippers. In one hand was a twisted cane. He must have been standing there the whole time, watching me.

"Don't be worried," he said. "I wouldn't hurt a fly. They're too small."

"I . . . I'm sorry!" I stammered, my mouth still full of funnel cake. "I didn't know this was yours."

"No worries. Do you like it?"

"Very much," I said.

"Must be my secret ingredient," the guy said.

"What is it?" I asked.

"Brains."

Maybe he was making a joke. Maybe not. In any case, I spit the stuff out, choking on what was still in my throat.

"Yes," he continued, "brains are quite a sought-after delicacy in many parts of the world. Makes sense, doesn't it? Eating brains should make you smarter. Too bad you weren't smart enough to not eat them. Because those who eat the brains must in turn have *their* brains eaten."

He took another step toward me.

"But I don't want my brains eaten!" I shouted, shrinking into the corner. "I just want to go home! I'll be late for lacrosse tryouts!" I wished Lionel was with me. He would know what to do.

"I'm sorry," the guy said, stopping suddenly. "How rude of me. I neglected to introduce myself. Professor Psycho, at your service."

He extended his hand, but I didn't shake it.

"Your name is *Professor Psycho*?!" I asked.

"Well, it's more of a nickname, actually," he said. "My real name is Milo DeVenus. I've been expecting you."

"You have?"

"You *are* Trip Dinkleman, right?"

"Yes," I admitted.

"You signed up to be part of my experiment, didn't you?"

"No," I told him. "I was just at the book fair and this stack of books fell and—"

"No matter," Professor Psycho said. "There was a form that came home in your backpack last week. Your mother must have filled it out. Mothers do that. Always looking out for their children. Perhaps if *my* mother had done that for *me*, things wouldn't have turned out the way they did."

"What did your mother do to you?"

"She gave me nothing but funnel cake to eat

for eight years," he said, a faraway look in his eye. "I went into an advanced state of sugar shock. It was quite horrible, actually. How ironic it is that so much of a good thing can be so bad for you. Everything in moderation, that's what they always say."

"I really need to go home," I said.

"Don't you want to hear my psychotic plan?" Professor Psycho asked.

"Maybe some other time," I said, backing toward the door.

"The human body is much like an automobile," he explained, ignoring me. "Both are made up of many separate parts that work together. When a car breaks down, we can simply order a new part to fix it. Presumably, we can just keep replacing parts as they wear out, and the car will run indefinitely. Why can't we do the same with human beings?"

"That's really interesting," I said, moving toward

where I thought I had come in. The door was gone. "But I really need to get home."

"We already have heart transplants and liver transplants," he went on, "why not a complete set of interchangeable body parts? It would allow us to live *forever*!"

I looked for a door, a hallway, anything that would get me out of there.

"Forget about cosmetic surgery," he continued. "You want a nose job? Just drop in and get an entirely new nose! You'll be able to order it from a catalog! I'll open a chain of human parts stores. It will be bigger than McDonald's. We'll have drive-through windows. Billions and billions served! Ahahahahahahaha!"

His evil cackling laugh reverberated off the walls of the old house. *This is just a bad dream*, I tried to convince myself.

"You're not real," I told him, as I took a few hesitant steps forward. "You're some kind of special effect. If you were real, I could just reach out and touch you."

"Go ahead then."

I reached my hand toward him, expecting to be able to poke my finger right through him. But I didn't get the chance. He grabbed my finger with his hand.

"I could use one of these," he said, and then he did that evil cackling laugh again before he let go of my finger.

"You're insane!" I shouted.

"Was Edison insane?" Professor Psycho shouted gleefully. "How about Einstein? Some call it insanity. I prefer to think of myself as . . . a divergent thinker."

"Look, mister," I yelled, "what you are is crazy, and I'm getting out of here."

I bolted past him into the same hallway I had come in from, but I wasn't more than a yard past the door when somebody tackled me. He was a horrible, disgusting, hideous-looking monster, his face bent and distorted in a tortured, grotesque mask of disfigurement. And I wasn't looking in any fun-house mirror this time.

"Arghhhhhhhh!" the thing grunted, as it picked me up like a feather and slammed me down in one of the kitchen chairs.

"This is my assistant, Ivan," Professor Psycho said. "He fled Estonia before the fall of the Soviet Union. Say hello to our guest, Ivan."

It didn't look as if Ivan was capable of human speech.

"Ivan was one of my early experiments," Professor Psycho continued. "Sadly, his face transplant didn't turn out exactly as planned."

"Let me go!" I screamed, as Ivan stretched a rope around my chest and tied it to the chair.

"The problem is that it's so hard to find attractive donors," Professor Psycho said.

"You'll never get away with this!" I yelled. "My parents will be here any minute!"

"That's what they all say," he said, chuckling. "Relax, Mr. Dinkleman. This won't take long. Ivan will be carrying out the actual procedure. I prefer to watch on my Webcam. Things can get . . . uh, messy, and I detest the sight of blood. Good luck, Trip."

With that, he hobbled away with his cane. I struggled to get out of the ropes, but Ivan had tied me up tightly. He opened the kitchen drawer, but instead of knives and forks and spoons, he took out all kinds of weird medical instruments and put them on the kitchen table.

"Look, Ivan," I said to him. "I'm sorry about your botched face transplant. That Professor Psycho guy is nuts. You don't need to stay with him. Let's get out of here! What do you say? You and me, together."

"Arghhhhhhhh!" Ivan grunted. He picked up a long sharp thing from the table and held it over my face. I shrank back in the chair.

He was about to cut me when a door slammed. The next thing I knew, a girl burst into the kitchen. This was no ordinary girl. She was beautiful, with long blond hair and blue eyes.

She had one of those laser pointers in her hand. She pushed a button and directed the beam at Ivan's face. Smoke started pouring out of his head, and he dropped the knife instantly. He grabbed his face and ran out of the room, screaming all the way down the hall.

"Who are you?" I asked the girl. "How did you get in here?"

"My name is Carrie," she said. "We're going to save you!"

"We?" I asked. "Who are we?"

"The Resistance," she replied.

"Where's Professor Psycho?"

"I killed him," Carrie told me. "You don't have to worry about him anymore. I've got to check on the others. Wait here; I'll be right back."

"No, don't go!" I called after her. "Untie me first!"

"No time for that!" she said, as she ran out of the room.

I had to cut the ropes, and fast. That Ivan lunatic could be coming back any second to finish me off himself. The knife he had dropped was still on the table, just out of my reach. Grunting, I slid the chair over so it was closer to the table. I leaned over, and picked up the knife in my mouth. Being careful not to cut myself, I rubbed the knife against the rope on my hand until the rope broke. My hands free, it was easy to take off the rest of the ropes. I ran out of the kitchen, down the hall, down the steps, out the door, and . . .

Where was I?

The boardwalk was gone! The haunted house was still there, but now it was out in the country, out in the middle of nowhere. There was a full moon in the sky. Off in the distance, an owl hooted and thunder clapped in applause.

This was *weird*. I hoped I was dreaming.

"Mr. Dinkleman!"

I turned around. It was Professor Psycho!

"I guess I'm just going to have to do your face transplant myself," he said, as he hobbled toward me.

I could outrun the guy, easy. I mean, he was walking with a cane. But there was a bike leaning against the fence. I could make a faster getaway on it.

I hopped on the bike and started pedaling, but the pedals wouldn't turn. Something was wrong. I looked down to see the chain had slipped off the gear. Professor Psycho was getting closer.

"Where's Carrie?" I shouted. "What did you do to her?"

"I want your face," he moaned. "Give me your face!"

I tossed the bike aside and took off on foot, running as fast as I could. The branches of the bushes on either side whipped me in the face as I ran past them. The ground was uneven, and my foot caught on something—a root maybe. I didn't see it coming. The next thing I knew, I was in the dirt.

"Leaving so soon, Trip?" Professor Psycho said. "We were just starting to have fun."

He was standing right over me now, holding some weird medical instrument.

"I thought you were dead!" I shouted.

"The reports of my death were, shall we say, exaggerated."

"Please!" I begged. "Don't hurt me."

"I tried to be reasonable with you, Trip. But my patience has worn thin. Face it; it's time to face the music. It's all about supply and demand. You have a face, and I need a face. So face the facts. This is no time to save face."

"Please!" I begged. "No more face puns."

Professor Psycho was waving his weird medical instrument over my head.

"Noooooooooo!" I screamed.

I put both hands up in the air to shield my face.

Chapter 3

Sports Fiction

The Game on the Line

I put both hands up in the air to shield my face. A guy in a football jersey slapped his palms against mine.

"Yeeeee-haaaaaaaaa!" shouted the player who high-fived me. "Dink, you *rule*!"

Huh?

The guy looked vaguely familiar to me. He was wearing a green Philadelphia Eagles football jersey. I looked down. So was I.

What the heck was going on?

I didn't have a whole lot of time to think about it, because a few seconds later the rest of the Eagles had run over and were jumping on me, pounding me, and telling me I was The Man. Photographers swarmed around, blinding me with flashes. A stadium full of people were on their feet screaming.

"Dinkleman! Dinkleman! Dinkleman! Dinkleman!"

"Dink," yelled the guy who high-fived me, "that was the awesomest catch I've seen in my life!"

"What?"

"Look for yourself," he said, pointing at a giant screen in the corner of the stadium.

I watched as the ball was snapped, and the quarterback of the Eagles dropped back to pass. A guy on the other team—it looked like the Patriots—broke through the line and was about to tackle him, but the quarterback spun away and scrambled out of the pocket. Then he heaved a long bomb.

At that point the video slowed down so you could see the laces turning as the ball arched toward the end zone. The receiver left his feet and dove—

full extension—catching the ball with his fingertips a couple of inches above the ground. Somehow, he held on to it even though he was creamed immediately by the guy covering him.

After he caught it, the receiver got up, looking a little dazed, and spiked the ball. One of his teammates ran over and gave him a high five. Then he just stood there in the end zone. Like me, standing there in the end zone.

I touched my nose. The guy on the screen touched his nose. I stuck out my tongue. The guy on the screen stuck out his tongue. I turned around. It said DINKLEMAN on the back of the guy's uniform.

The guy on the screen was *me*!

I was still woozy. Two of the Eagles put their arms around me and helped me to the sideline.

"Where's Professor Psycho?" I asked them. "Where's the funnel cake?"

"Professor *Who*?" one of the guys said. "Are you okay, Dinkleman? We need you, man. This is the Super Bowl!"

"That hit on the head scrambled his brains."

"You remember me, right, Dink?" said the guy who had first high-fived me. "Lionel? We've been best friends since we were kids. I was your backup on the high school team. I was your backup in college. And now we're on the Eagles together. Right?"

I looked at the guy. It *was* Lionel! He looked as if he was ten years older. What was *he* doing here? Something was seriously wrong.

In the stands, maybe eighty thousand people were giving me a standing ovation. But all I felt was a sense of relief. There was no haunted house here. No Professor Psycho performing bizarre medical experiments on me. No Ivan. I was big. I was strong. I had muscles. I would make an awesome lacrosse player.

I felt my face. I had a mustache. But it felt like *my* face. I didn't have a face transplant.

"Dinkleman! Dinkleman! Dinkleman!"

"We love you, Trip!"

I looked up at the scoreboard.

PHILADELPHIA 27
NEW ENGLAND 24

Fourth quarter. My miraculous catch must have put the Eagles ahead.

"Coach, I think Dink needs some help!" Lionel told a guy who was wearing street clothes and headphones. "He may have had a concussion."

"Dinkleman, how many fingers am I holding up?" the coach asked me.

"All of them," I replied.

They lowered me to the bench and somebody handed me a glass of water.

"Trip, you've done all you could for us," the

coach told me. "You're finished for the day. Lionel! If we get the ball again, I'm gonna need you in there at wide receiver."

"Yes sir!" Lionel said, putting on his helmet.

Our kicker kicked the extra point to make it 28–24. The Patriots returned the kickoff to their 40-yard line. There were three minutes left on the clock, and the Patriot quarterback didn't waste a second of it. He completed a series of quick short passes to the sidelines and stopped the clock when his receivers stepped out of bounds.

A field goal wasn't going to beat us. The Patriots needed to score a touchdown or we would be Super Bowl champions.

The clock was ticking down. They had the ball on our 20-yard line when their quarterback faked a handoff, rolled right, and took off down the sideline. A few good blocks and a few missed tackles later, he was diving into the end zone.

PHILADELPHIA 28
NEW ENGLAND 30

The Patriots kicked the extra point to make it 31–28. The two-minute warning was given. Automatic time-out. What had been euphoria on the Eagles bench had turned into gloom. The coach gathered us all around him in a huddle.

"You remember what happened to us last season, right?" he said. "We finished 0 and 16. Remember the game where the Packers humiliated us 64–0?"

The players nodded their heads solemnly.

"And you know what happened to us this season, right?" he continued. "We went 16 and 0. We went from worst to first!"

"Worst to first! Worst to first!" the players chanted.

"And do you know *why* we went from worst to first?" the coach asked.

"'Cause we worked our butts off!" Lionel shouted.

"Yeah, that had a lot to do with it," the coach agreed. "What else?"

"Was it because the Green Bay Packer bus went over a cliff and killed half the team?" some other guy shouted.

"That had a lot to do with it too," said the coach. "And what else?"

"Those aliens came and gave us special powers," some other guy said.

"Yeah, that helped too," said the coach. "But I think we all know the number one reason why we're here playing in the Super Bowl today. It's because of Coach Lip."

Everybody bowed his head. Some were sniffling.

"There's no need for me to go back and rehash the tragic Frisbee accident at Hoover Dam," the coach said. "We all know what happened."

"The coach had that Frisbee in his hands," Lionel said.

"And we've got this game in our hands," the coach said. "We can grab it. Or we can drop it. That's going to be up to you. But whatever you do, let's dedicate these last two minutes to Coach Lip. Let's win this one for the Lipper."

"Lipper! Lipper! Lipper! Lipper!"

We returned the kickoff to our 35-yard line. Decent field position. But we knew we weren't going to be trying for a field goal to tie it up. Oh, no. We were going for the six points. We were going for the win.

Our offense moved the ball to the 45, to midfield, to the Patriots' 30-yard line. Lionel, who had replaced me, made a couple of good catches. But the clock was ticking down. There were thirty seconds left, and the goal line was still so far away.

The team went into a hurry-up offense and snapped the ball while the Patriots were still setting up their defense. Lionel raced down the left side-line. The quarterback whipped the ball to him at the twenty. He caught it, faking out one defender and dashing to the ten. He was hit hard there by two guys, and he collapsed to the ground. Lionel didn't get up. There were five seconds left on the clock when the coach called time.

We all ran out to help. Lionel was holding his leg and moaning.

"I think it's broken!" he cried.

They carried Lionel off the field on a stretcher. But we couldn't focus on him now. There were five seconds left in the Super Bowl, and we had the ball on the seven-yard line.

"Trip, can you go out there?" the coach asked me.

"Me?" I said, as the Eagle team doctor came over.

"Dinkleman has a probable concussion," the doctor told the coach. "He should not set foot on this field. He should be in the hospital with Lionel. If Trip goes in there and gets a good shot to the head again, well, he might be permanently brain damaged."

"What do you want to do, Trip?" the coach asked me.

"I . . . uh . . . ," I mumbled, "want to go home."

"He is obviously in no position to make this decision!" warned the doctor.

"Okay," said the coach. "We'll let his wife make the decision."

"My *wife*?!"

At that moment, this pretty blond girl was brought over. Wait a minute! I recognized her. She was the girl who had rescued me from Professor Psycho at the haunted house! It was Carrie! She was my wife?!

"Are you okay, honey?" she asked, cradling my head in her hands.

"Uh, yeah," I told her. "Do you still have that cool laser pointer?"

"Laser pointer?" she asked. "What are you talking about?"

"He's delirious, Mrs. Dinkleman," said the doctor.

"Trip, look at me," Carrie said, as I gazed into her deep blue eyes. "The guys need you now. Every man on this team has worked and struggled and practiced so hard for so long. And it all leads up to this moment. Do you think you can pull yourself together for just one more play?"

"I'll try."

"That's my man," she said. "You can go to the hospital *after* the game."

When they saw me coming out to the huddle, the crowd erupted.

"Dinkleman! Dinkleman! Dinkleman! Dinkleman!"

"This is it, guys," the quarterback said. "Win

NIGHTMARE AT THE BOOK FAIR

or lose. Make or break. It all comes down to this. Red . . . 49 . . .left . . . triangle. On two. Got it?"

"Uh, not exactly," I said.

"Don't you remember the plays, Trip?"

"His brain is fried from that hit he took," said one of the other players.

"It's simple," the quarterback told me. "I'm going to fake the handoff to Ronnie and give it to you instead. Follow him right up the middle. It's seven yards. Ronnie will clear the path, and you jump over the pile if you need to. Nothing fancy."

"But I thought I was a receiver," I said.

"You are," he said. "This will completely fool them."

We clapped hands and came out of the huddle.

"24 . . . 21 . . . 2 . . . hut . . . hut . . . hut . . ."

The quarterback took the snap, wheeled around, and faked the handoff to Ronnie. I followed right behind him, looking in front for a hole to run through. I felt something hard jammed into my gut.

Chapter 4

Adventure

Sixty Seconds to Live

I felt something hard jammed into my gut. It was a fist.

"*Oooooooff!*" I grunted, falling backward and landing in a pile of boxes.

Frantically, I looked around. I was in a small plane. It was one of those twelve seaters, except that there were no seats. That was odd.

The plane was humming and rumbling, bumping through turbulence. I looked for something to grab on to.

"Have you had enough, Dinkleman?"

The guy who had punched me was standing there. He was wearing a military uniform and punching one fist into an open palm.

He was looking straight at me, but there was so much noise that I wasn't sure who he was talking to. I looked around to see if anybody was behind me. Nobody was there.

"Did we win the Super Bowl?" I asked.

The guy didn't answer. Instead, he pulled on a large red handle, which opened the door on the side of the plane. A whoosh of wind rushed in, and some papers swirled around. Outside, grayish clouds were shooting by.

"Jump, Dinkleman!"

"Me?"

I don't *think* so. I've never parachuted before. It's something that I've always thought would be interesting to try. I should take some lessons. Maybe someday.

"Yeah, you! Or would you like another shot to the gut?"

This guy was creepy looking, with a mustache

that almost perfectly matched his unibrow. It was like an optical illusion on his face—which line was longer? He took a step closer to me with every word he spoke. When he was a foot away, I realized he was wearing a disguise. I recognized that face.

"Lionel!" I said. "What are you doing here? What happened at the Super Bowl? Why did you punch me?"

"My name is Murphy," Lionel said.

"This is all a big joke, right, Lionel?" I said. "What, is it April Fools' Day or something?"

"Enough fooling around! I said *jump*, Dinkleman!"

"Well, if you're not my best friend Lionel, then how do you know my name?" I asked.

"It's right there on your uniform, you idiot!"

I looked down. He was right. I was wearing a camouflage outfit with my name embroidered on a patch on my chest.

"You go ahead, Lionel," I told him. "I'll be

right behind you. I'm just going to tidy up in here a bit."

"*Now*, Dinkleman! And stop calling me Lionel. Don't make me get rough with you."

Make him? If I was going to make him do anything, it would be leave me alone.

"But I'm afraid of heights," I said. "I don't even like Ferris wheels. You know that. Look, I just want to go home. Remember? We were going to try out for lacrosse."

"Don't worry about going home, Dinkleman," the guy who looked like Lionel said. "In sixty seconds, you'll be on the ground."

"After you, I insist," I said, gesturing for him to go first.

"You think I'm fooling around here?!" he thundered. And with that, he pulled a gun out of his waistband and pointed it at my head. "Get *out*!"

Whoa!

"Okay, I get it," I said, sweating profusely.

"Where's my parachute? Will you at least show me how to work it?"

"Parachute?" he said, sticking his chin in my face and forcing me to stand up to him or take a step back toward the open door. I took a step back. "Parachutes are for crybabies!"

"Why are you trying to kill me, Lionel?" I stuttered. "We're best friends! Wh-what did I do?"

"You know perfectly well what you did, Dinkleman!" he said. "Don't play dumb."

I wasn't playing dumb. I *was* dumb.

"Th-there must be some misunderstanding," I explained. "I never did anything to anybody. You must have mistaken me for somebody who looks like me. Just like you look like Lionel. Please, can't we just talk about it?"

"The time for talk is over!" he said, cocking the gun. "It's your choice. Die now, or die later."

Jumping out of a plane without a parachute meant certain death. Staying up there in the plane with this lunatic who looked like Lionel meant highly probable death. Given the choice, I'd pick highly probable death over certain death any day of the week.

"No!" I said, trying to look brave. "I'm not going to—"

Before I could say another word, he picked up his boot, rammed it into my stomach, and shoved me backward through the open door.

"Ahhhhhhhhhhhhhhhhhhhhhhhhhhh!" I screamed. "Heeellllllllllllllllppppppppp!"

This was totally not fair! I didn't do anything! All I did was go to a stupid book fair. And now I was falling out of a plane without a parachute and I was going to die!

The wind tore at my skin, my face, my hair as I tumbled backward, flailing with my arms and legs to try and stabilize myself. I never stopped screaming.

My eyes were tearing and I couldn't see a thing. Just whiteness all around as I fell through a cloud.

The air was cold. The plane was long gone.

"Heeeeeeeeeeelllllllllllllllllp!"

It was pointless. My brief life was over. I'd never had the chance to drive a car. Never had a job. Never did anything meaningful. What a waste. I resolved right there that, if by some miracle, I survived this thing, I would never go to another book fair again.

There was a break in the clouds, but I couldn't see the ground. I didn't *want* to see the ground. But then, suddenly, there was an opening and some fields and forests came into view.

"Ahhhhhhhhhhhhhhhhhhhhhhhhhhhh! I'm gonna dieeeeeeeeeeeeeee!"

That's when somebody grabbed me from behind.

I turned my head around. It was Carrie, the beautiful blond girl who had saved me from Professor Psycho and had been my wife at the Super Bowl!

"I gotcha, Trip!" she said.

"What are *you* doing here?" I yelled.

"What does it look like I'm doing?" she asked. "Saving your life! Grab hold of me!"

I wrapped my arms around Carrie. She had a parachute on her back.

"Why did that guy push me out of the plane?"

"Let me give you some exposition," she explained.

"Expo-what?"

"Exposition," she replied. "That's when a story-teller explains everything that led up to the present events. You see, it all started with your great-grandfather Harry, who owned a farm in Yugoslavia. There was another man who lived next door. He and your grandfather got into an argument one day over some potatoes."

The ground was starting to look a lot closer. Something told me that falling out of a plane was probably not the best time to be giving exposition.

"Could you finish the exposition later?" I suggested. "I think you should open up your parachute now."

"It's very important to explain the depth and psychological aspects of your being," she said. "It gives meaning and depth to the story. Otherwise, you're just some kid who got pushed out of a plane. Nobody cares about that."

"I do!" I shouted.

"So anyway," she continued, "the other guy stole your great-grandfather's wife and ran away, which made your grandfather go on a worldwide quest to get his revenge and win back the heart of your great-grandmother. Years and years went by—"

Luckily for me, this was the longest sixty seconds ever recorded in history. But even so, the ground was coming up fast.

"Shut up!" I yelled. "Open the parachute!"

She pulled a cord, and I braced myself to be

jolted upward as the chute opened. But there was no jolt. No nothing.

"It's not opening!" she yelled in my ear. "Something must be wrong!"

"It must have been sabotaged by that guy who looks like Lionel or Professor Psycho!" I yelled in her ear.

"Professor *Who*?" she yelled back.

"Forget it," I yelled. "Do you have a backup chute?"

"Yes!"

"Thank goodness!"

"It's back up in the plane!" she yelled.

"I can't believe you're making jokes at a time like this!" I yelled.

"I'm not making a joke," she yelled back. "The backup chute really *is* back up in the plane!"

My breath caught in my throat. That's it. Unless we were able to come up with a completely improbable and far-fetched solution to the mess we were in, we were both going to die.

"Wait!" Carrie yelled. "I happen to suddenly remember there's a conveniently placed cotton candy factory almost directly below us! If I can maneuver us to the right about a hundred yards, we'll crash through the glass roof and land on about a hundred tons of cotton candy! It will break our fall!"

What luck!

We were low enough now that I could see individual buildings. And there it was! On the roof of the big building directly below us were the words COLEMAN'S COTTON CANDY. We were heading straight for it.

"Ready?" Carrie shouted in my ear.

"Yeah!"

"Set?"

"Yeah!"

"Hold on!"

"I'm holding on!"

"Brace yourself!"

"I'm bracing myself!"

I closed my eyes, took a deep breath, and we crashed through the glass. I wasn't sure if I was dead or alive.

Chapter 5
Science Fiction

The Good Samaritans

I wasn't sure if I was dead or alive. The sky was a deep blue, bluer than seemed possible in the real world. I stared at it as I lay on my back in the grass. I was safe. Nobody was trying to kill me. Nobody was trying to steal my face or push me out of a plane. The sun was warming. All was well on planet Earth.

I turned my head to the left and saw . . . the Washington Monument. I turned my head to the right and saw . . . the United States Capitol building. Well, at least I knew where I was for a change—smack in the middle of the National Mall in Washington, DC. I had seen it on TV plenty of times, but I'd never been there.

"Hey Dink!" somebody yelled. "Are you okay, man?"

I looked up. It was Lionel! And there was my social studies teacher, Mrs. Babcock! And the other kids in my class at school! My nightmare must be over.

"Lionel!" I shouted. "Why did you push me out of that plane?"

Everybody cracked up.

"Uh," Lionel said, "maybe because you stole my little bag of peanuts?"

"I guess I just dozed off and had a bad dream," I said. "Why are we in Washington?"

"It's the class trip, silly boy!" said Mrs. Babcock, laughing, as she extended a hand to help me up. "Come on, we're late for the tour of the Capitol."

My whole class was milling around the grass, walking slowly toward the Capitol building. I fell in with Lionel, not saying much. It would take a while to get used to the idea that I was in the real world again.

The other kids were talking about the trip. I didn't remember any of it. They pretty much agreed that Ford's Theater was the best thing they'd seen so far. The Lincoln Memorial and the Holocaust Museum were really interesting, but the International Spy Museum wasn't nearly as cool as everybody had thought it was going to be. Everybody apparently wanted to go to the White House but decided not to because the President was visiting Portugal this week and he wouldn't be there.

We passed the National Air and Space Museum on our right. I knew it was filled with planes, rockets, and relics from the space program—everything from the Wright brothers' plane to a Hubble telescope.

"You know what would be awesome?" Lionel said. "If a UFO landed here, right outside the Air and Space Museum."

"That would never happen," one of the other kids said. "Did you ever notice that UFOs are never spotted where lots of people would see them? They never land in New York City or Chicago. They only show up in some cornfield in the middle of nowhere and places where the only witnesses are nuts, drunks, and UFO fanatics."

It was true. If aliens with superior intelligence *really* wanted to contact us, the perfect place to do it would be the middle of the nation's capitol.

We were all laughing about that when I saw the flash in the sky.

It was a color I'd never seen before. I know the colors of the visual spectrum. I know all about Roy G. Biv (red, orange, yellow, green, blue, indigo, violet). But this was a new color. It was indescribable.

After the flash and a brilliant afterimage came a boom, billowing smoke, and the smell of sulfur in the air. The smoke began to clear, and bright white lights poked through the haze. We all just stared, transfixed. Soon I could make out a shape. It wasn't like the saucer-shape spaceships you see in comic books. It was more like a tire from a car, lying on its side. A tire about the size of a building.

My first reaction was that it had to be some advertising campaign. Or maybe somebody was shooting a movie. Maybe we were going to be on TV.

But it was all too real.

"Holy—," Lionel said.

We froze, but a lot of the other tourists scattered, running wildly toward the museums that line the mall. Lights began to blink on the ship as it hovered about ten feet off the ground. The grass directly underneath it appeared to turn blue.

"Everybody stay calm," Mrs. Babcock whispered, as we instinctively gathered around her for protection. "Don't make any sudden moves."

A few kids grabbed for cameras and cell phones to take pictures. Nobody could take their eyes off the ship, but everybody was whispering questions, as if any of us knew the answers.

"What should we do?"

"Why are they here?"

"What kind of weapons do they have?"

"Are we going to die?"

Me, I just had one question—when would we be able to go home?

A low buzzing sound seemed to move from left to right. Then a disk, about the size of a Hula Hoop, lowered from the middle of the ship. And standing on the disk was some sort of—creature.

It had legs—three of them supporting itself like a tripod. The body of the thing looked almost human, except that it was covered with a shiny metallic surface. It didn't appear to be armor or clothing. It was the outside of the creature. The thing itself was about seven feet tall.

We all gasped as it raised one arm. It had no fingers.

The head, if you can call it a head, was octagonally shaped, with no hair and no nose. It did have a mouth, a gaping hole with no lips. The eyes— four of them—were about three times larger than human eyes, and they scanned our faces in a sideways motion. It was unclear to me whether or not we were being photographed.

It didn't talk or gesture. It just stood there looking back at us. But somehow, I felt the words inside my head as if I was listening to an iPod.

"We are from the planet Samar," it told me. "We have traveled a hundred thousand light years to see for ourselves."

Aliens!

"To see *what* for yourselves?" asked Mrs. Babcock, taking a hesitant step forward.

So we were *all* hearing the voice!

"I must speak to your leader," the thing echoed in my head.

"Our leader is out of the country," Mrs. Babcock

said. "We have three branches of government. The executive, the legislature, and the judic—"

"Who is in charge?" the thing demanded, with more urgency, it seemed.

We all looked toward the Capitol, and the thing turned on its disk to face the huge building.

"Let us go there," it said.

Word must have spread. A siren wailed in the distance. There were helicopters in the air. I could see guys inside holding guns. I was sure they would have opened fire on the alien if there weren't so many of us kids in the way.

The alien on the disk slid forward along the grass toward the Capitol building. I didn't make a conscious effort to follow, but something was pulling me along. Something was pulling *all* of us along, and soon we were running to keep up with it.

"Don't shoot it!" Mrs. Babcock yelled, as the Capitol security police gathered outside the building with their guns drawn. A shot rang out anyway, but it didn't hit the alien. He raised his hand and a beam of something—maybe light—shot out to stop the bullet in midair. It bounced harmlessly to the ground near me. When I picked it up, it was freezing. These aliens must be able to shoot microwaves or some freezing equivalent of microwaves.

"Do not put your children at risk!" the alien said.

It led our whole class inside the Capitol. It seemed to know where it was going. The security guards just stood there watching, terrified. They weren't about to risk killing one of us in cross fire.

The alien led us into a huge room. I had seen it on TV. This was the room where Congress gathered to debate and vote on laws. The senators must have been notified of the disturbance. When we entered the room, a group of old guys in suits and ties turned and stared at the creature, terror in their eyes.

"Who are you?" one of them asked. "Why are you here?"

The thing didn't speak, but each and every one of us heard it anyway.

"We have come to warn you," it said. "There is a grave threat to your civilization. If you do not address it immediately, your planet will become uninhabitable."

All the senators started to buzz with conversation.

"Is it an asteroid?" asked one of the senators.

"No."

"Bird flu pandemic?" asked another.

"No," the thing said. "The threat is from within."

"What is this, some kind of joke?" one of the senators asked.

"We have been observing you," the alien responded. "You burn twenty million barrels of oil every day. In the last century, you burned most of the oil that your planet took millions of years to create."

"That's none of your business," one of the senators said.

"True," the thing replied. "It is *your* business. The last ten years were the hottest decade in your history. Does that not tell you anything? Your atmosphere has heated up to the point that your polar ice caps are melting. Water levels are rising. Species are becoming extinct. Soon the oil will be depleted, and your planet will be uninhabitable."

"Look, we know global warming is a problem," a senator stepped forward and said. "We're studying it, evaluating various solutions, courses of action. This doesn't happen overnight. A blue ribbon panel has been appointed, and in time—"

"You are running out of time!" the alien said. "The time to study is past. The time to act is now. In this spirit, the people of Samar offer a gift."

Then, he produced a box. I don't know where it came from. I didn't see the thing reach into a pocket or anything. It didn't have any pockets. It just produced a box out of thin air. The box was small, about the size of a tissue box.

"What is it?" a senator asked. None of them were rushing forward to accept the gift.

"It contains a pellet," the alien said. "We have developed a source of power strong enough to meet the energy needs of your planet for a thousand years."

"That's bull!" yelled one of the senators.

"Impossible!" yelled another.

"What arc you supposed to do with the spent fuel?" a third senator asked. "Where do we store the waste?"

"There *is* no waste," the thing said. "No greenhouse gases. No pollution. No negative side effects."

"It sounds like an infomercial to me," one of the senators near us muttered. "What's the catch?"

"When a civilization is in trouble as yours obviously is, we are duty bound to offer any assistance we can," said the alien.

"I suppose in exchange for this pellet you get to rule us," said a senator. "Is that the way you work this scam?"

"We ask for nothing," said the alien.

"We must confer," one of the senators announced. "This is a democracy. We need time to talk it over."

"Be quick. Time is your enemy."

The creature moved to the far end of the chamber, while the senators squeezed into the opposite corner of the room, where we were standing. I could hear every word they said.

"I don't trust this guy, if it *is* a guy."

"This pellet thing, if it works, would put the oil and energy companies out of business."

"Gas stations too."

"We'd have to revamp our entire energy system

and redesign it from the ground up."

"The automobile industry would freak out."

"It will hurt the economy."

". . . lose jobs."

"If we stop buying oil, it will set off a world-wide financial crisis."

"I come up for re-election in November. I don't need this aggravation."

"That thing has got a lot of nerve, coming here and telling us how we should run things."

"He should mind his own business."

"Who knows what's in that box? Maybe it's a bomb. How did that thing get past security?"

"Nobody travels a hundred thousand light years out of the kindness of his heart."

"He's trying to control us. That's his scheme. Trust me, he'll have us worshipping him in no time."

"It's a trick."

"It's a trap."

"If they can get that much energy into a pellet,

can you imagine the weapons they have? He could snap his fingers and wipe us out. That is, if he had fingers."

"I say we blow him to kingdom come."

"Yeah, let's kill him now, while we have the chance."

Kill him? I huddled close to my classmates, as if that would provide any protection once the bullets started flying. I was safer in the haunted house. I was safer when I was falling out of that plane.

One of the senators, who had been standing in the back and had not said anything, suddenly spoke up. He was an older man, with glasses.

"Has it occurred to any of you," he said, "that maybe this alien is making sense? Maybe we should listen to him."

All eyes turned to look at him.

"Hey, whose side are you on, Whitney? Are you with us or against us?" one of the senators said.

"How do we know Senator Whitney isn't in

cahoots with the alien?" said another. "For that matter, how do we know he isn't an alien posing as one of us?"

"They've infiltrated the government!"

A couple of the senators grabbed the one they called Senator Whitney and put him in a choke hold.

"Let's vote on it," one of the senators said. "All in favor of killing the alien, say aye."

"Aye," virtually all of them said.

"All opposed?"

Senator Whitney struggled to speak. Otherwise, there was silence.

"Majority rules," said the senator who had conducted the vote. "That's the beauty of democracy."

The senators, as a group, went back to the other side of the huge room, where the alien was waiting patiently.

"We have a response for you," one of the senators said.

With that, he pulled a gun out of his jacket and fired it at the alien. I expected to see the alien collapse, or at least get knocked backward from the blow, but it didn't even react.

"You missed!" one of the senators shouted. "Shoot him again!"

The senator fired again, and again there was no reaction from the alien. The senator pumped out the remaining bullets in his gun with the same effect. The bullets, instead of hitting the alien, were ricocheting around the room. We all hit the floor.

"I just want to go home!" Lionel groaned.

"Me too!" I replied.

"The alien has put up some kind of a force field!" one of the senators hollered. "Let's get him!"

As a group, the senators charged at the alien. But as soon as they got within five feet of it, they screamed and fell to the ground. It was as if they had run into an invisible brick wall. They were all over the floor, moaning in pain.

"I anticipated this response," said the alien. "Any civilization that would purposefully waste its natural resources and gradually destroy itself with no thought about the consequences clearly lacks the intelligence necessary for long-term survival."

"Wh-what are you going to do to us?" one of the senators asked.

"Put you out of your misery," was all it said. Then it opened the box it had been holding. A blinding yellow light shot out. The floor started rumbling. The lights above began vibrating. Chunks of plaster started falling from the roof. The building was breaking apart. Something struck me on the head.

Chapter 6

Humor

The Continuing Adventures of Captain Obvious and the Exaggerator

Something struck me on the head. And then, I farted.

It was one of those loud smelly ones that rattles the windows and clears a room. But I wasn't in a room. I was outside. It looked as if I was in the middle of a cornfield or something.

"Say, who cut the cheese?" somebody asked.

I looked up, which is basically the only place you can look when you're flat on your back. There were two guys standing over me. One of them had a big letter *O* on his chest. The other one had a big *E*. And they were both wearing tights.

Now, when you see grown men wearing tights,

it can only mean one of two things. Either they're ballet dancers, or they happen to be guys who just enjoy wearing tights. However, there was a third possibility that had not even entered my mind.

"We are Captain Obvious and the Exaggerator, the dynamic duo!" they said in unison.

"And I am Captain Obvious!" said the one with the big O on his chest.

"I guessed that because of the big O on your chest," I told him.

"Obviously!" said Captain Obvious.

"And, by the process of elimination," said the other guy, "I must be the Exaggerator, the greatest superhero in the history of mankind."

"Really?" I asked.

"Well, no," said the Exaggerator. "To be perfectly honest, that was somewhat of an exaggeration."

"I'm Trip Dinkleman," I said, as they helped me up.

"Our job is to fight evil," said Captain Obvious.

"Duh!" I said. "Isn't that what *all* super-heroes do?"

"I felt it needed to be said," Captain Obvious said.

"We use our power of exaggeration and pointing out the obvious to defeat evildoers and make the world safe for humanity," said the Exaggerator. "We are the number one fictional crime-fighting superhero team in the world."

"What about Batman and Robin?" I asked.

"Well, maybe we're number two," admitted the Exaggerator.

"You appear to have taken a nasty spill there, young fellow," said Captain Obvious. "What happened?"

"Well, it all started when I was at my school book fair—"

"Stop right there!" interrupted Captain Obvious. "Is a book fair some sort of a fair where books are sold?"

"Uh, yeah," I told him. "And something fell on my head."

"I bet it was a two-ton anvil!" said the Exaggerator.

"Obviously," said Captain Obvious.

"I don't think there are any anvils at my school," I told them.

"A safe?" asked the Exaggerator. "When something falls on someone's head in cartoons, it's usually a safe or an anvil."

"I doubt it."

"A piano maybe?"

"I think it was just some books," I told them.

"Of course!" said Captain Obvious, snapping his fingers. "He was at a book fair. It *had* to be books!"

They high-fived each other and seemed quite pleased with themselves.

"Anyway," I continued, "I guess it knocked me out or something, because I started having these weird hallucinations where I found myself in the middle of all these different kinds of books. In fact, I think I'm in the middle of one right now. All I want to do is go home so I can try out for the lacrosse team."

"That's the most incredible story I've ever heard!" said the Exaggerator.

"Really?"

"Uh, no," he admitted. "Not really."

"Do you have to exaggerate *everything*?" I asked him. "It's really annoying."

"If I didn't exaggerate everything, I couldn't very well call myself the Exaggerator, now, could I?" he asked.

"Obviously not," said Captain Obvious.

"Enough of this mindless introductory chit-chat," said the Exaggerator, as he grabbed my arm. "We need your help. You must join us on a life-or-death mission!"

"What?" I asked. "Why me?"

"The world, as we know it, is threatened!" said the Exaggerator.

"Wait a minute," I said. "Are you exaggerating?"

"Yes!" said the Exaggerator. "But we desperately need your help. Quickly, put this on!"

He handed me a costume. It looked a lot like their costumes, but it had a big letter *A* on the chest. I wasn't sure I wanted to know what the *A* stood for.

"From now on," said Captain Obvious, "you will be known as . . . The Alliterator!"

"I don't even know what that means," I said.

"*Alliterating* is saying a string of words that all begin with the same sound," said Captain Obvious.

"You mean, like Peter Piper picked a peck of pickled peppers?" I asked.

"See? He's doing it already!" said the Exaggerator. "Every single sentence you say must be an alliteration."

"Every single one?" I asked.

"Well, most of them."

Against my better judgment, I put the silly costume on. And do you know what? They were right! Something came over me almost instantly. I felt the power of alliteration surge through my body.

"Singing Sammy sung songs on sinking sand. Sunday smiles shine sunny signs of spring."

"I think he's got it!" said Captain Obvious. "Let's go!"

We hopped into the Exaggerator's car, which was low and black and had flames shooting out of the exhaust pipe. It was really cool.

"This baby can do three hundred miles per hour," claimed the Exaggerator.

"Really?"

"Well, not quite," he said. "But it goes really fast."

He was right about that. When he hit the gas, my head slammed against the headrest, and I felt the skin on my cheeks flapping in the breeze.

"Where are we going?" I asked.

"That's not very alliterative," said Captain Obvious.

"Which way will we wend?" I asked. "West?"

"Our mission is to apprehend the most dangerous and despicable supervillain in the world," the Exaggerator explained. "We understand that he is building a giant vacuum cleaner that will suck all the oxygen out of the atmosphere until humans can no longer breathe and we will all die."

"Rubber baby buggy bumpers!" I exclaimed.

"Nobody knows what this evil supervillain looks like," said Captain Obvious. "Nobody knows his name. But he has a secret hideout that is conveniently located not far from here."

We drove a few miles, and I knew we were getting close to the secret hideout when I saw a big sign at the side of the road that said, THIS WAY TO SECRET HIDEOUT.

"Won't he have gates and security and roadblocks

and stuff like that to prevent people like us from getting in?" I asked.

"No," Captain Obvious told me, "there's a parking lot right out front."

So there was. Finally, we reached the secret hideout. The Exaggerator flipped the keys to the parking attendant.

"How vill vee ever know ven vee view the very vicious villain?" I asked.

"It will be obvious," said Captain Obvious. "You hide in the bushes. We'll call you if we need backup."

He rang the bell, and a man opened the door. Peeking through the bushes, I recognized his face instantly. It was Professor Psycho, that lunatic who had tried to steal my face at the haunted house! What was *he* doing here? Was he now building a giant vacuum cleaner that would suck all the oxygen out of the atmosphere? And most importantly, why did he have a big letter *I* on the front of his shirt? Was it a disguise?

"Well, if it isn't Flotsam and Jetsam!" he said. "What a sight for sore eyes. You Goody-Two-shoes are like two peas in a pod. What's the matter, cat got your tongue?"

"This guy talks funny," said Captain Obvious.

"You hit the nail on the head, Captain O," said Professor Psycho. "They call me . . . Mr. Idiom."

"Idiom?" Captain Obvious asked. "What's that? An idiot with an *M*?"

"Ignorance is bliss, Obvious," said Mr. Idiom. "An *idiom* is a common expression whose meaning can't be understood from the individual words in it."

"Oh yeah?" said the Exaggerator. "Well, we know all about your secret plan to build a giant vacuum cleaner that will suck the air out of the atmosphere. We're going to put you away for a thousand years, Mr. Idiom."

"Don't count your chickens before they hatch," Mr. Idiom said, sneering.

"You are the most evil supervillain in the history of the world," said the Exaggerator, "and besides that, your breath smells like the rotting corpses of a million goats."

"Hold your horses," Mr. Idiom said, putting his arm around the Exaggerator. "You're making a mountain out of a molehill. Take a chill pill. Let's bury the hatchet and turn the other cheek. Don't get your dander up. There's no use crying over spilled milk. Let's not split hairs. Why burn your bridges?"

"Enough idioms already!" said Captain Obvious. "You're under arrest for attempting to suck up the earth's atmosphere and suffocate humanity."

"Oh, put a cork in it, Obvious," Mr. Idiom said. "It's time to stop beating around the bush, stop mincing words, and get down to brass tacks. I have a bone to pick with you two. Here's the bottom line. Your bark is worse than your bite, and you're full of hot air. You've got a chip on your shoulder, and you bit off more than you can chew. The hand-writing is on the wall. The chickens have come home to roost."

"Are you calling us chicken?" said Captain Obvious.

"If the shoe fits, wear it."

"You are a bad man!" said Captain Obvious, and then he punched Mr. Idiom right in the nose!

"Oh, that's the straw that broke the camel's back," Mr. Idiom said, holding his nose.

The next thing I knew, the three of them were fighting, punching, kicking, and rolling around on the ground.

"The sky is blue!" said Captain Obvious, as he tried to strangle Mr. Idiom. "You have two eyes!"

"Pointing out the obvious is no match for my endless arsenal of idioms," said Mr. Idiom. "So button your lip and eat your heart out!"

I figured that the number two fictional crime-fighting superhero team in the world would be able to beat up Mr. Idiom easily, but I was wrong. When the dust had cleared, Captain Obvious and the Exaggerator were sitting on the ground, back-to-back, with a rope tied around them.

"Now the shoe is on the other foot, eh?" Mr. Idiom said. "You know, you guys just rub me the wrong way. You've gotten too big for your britches. I'm tired of playing cat and mouse. It's time for you to face the music, pay the piper, fish or cut bait. And it's time for me to lower the boom."

"Are you going to kill us?" asked Captain Obvious.

"Oh, I'm going to kill two birds with one stone," Mr. Idiom said. "I'm going to strike while the iron is hot and fix your wagon. I'll pull out all the stops and make you eat your words. This is going to be a piece of cake."

"Stop!" the Exaggerator said, covering his ears. "Stop using so many idioms! I can't take it anymore! I think I'm getting a migraine."

"You'll never get away with this!" said Captain Obvious. "Bad guys always lose in the end."

"I've got you two over a barrel," Mr. Idiom said. "You missed the boat, and now you're up a creek without a paddle. It looks like you're between a rock and a hard place. I'm in the driver's seat now. Like it or lump it. You're behind the eight ball. From now on, I call the shots. It's time to give up the ghost. That's the way the cookie crumbles."

"Oh, my head!" moaned the Exaggerator. "Too many idioms! My brain is going to explode."

"Save us, Alliterator!" shouted Captain Obvious desperately. "You're our only hope!"

"Alliterator?" asked Mr. Idiom. "Who's that?"

I jumped out from behind the bushes and grabbed him.

"It is I!" I shouted. "The superhero do-gooder who speaks in alliterations. I slit the sheet, the sheet I slit, and on the slitted sheet I sit!"

A lot of good that did. Mr. Idiom, or Professor

Psycho, or whatever his name was, broke out of my hold and grabbed me right back. Within a minute I was tied up like the other two.

"I see you had an ace up your sleeve," Mr. Idiom told them. "Well, the Alliterator may have the gift of gab. But I'm top banana now. And what's good for the goose is good for the gander. It's a dog-eat-dog world."

Suddenly, out of nowhere, something dropped out of the sky and landed on Mr. Idiom. It was a man, and he had a big letter *L* on his chest.

"It's Lee Literal!" shouted Captain Obvious and the Exaggerator.

"That's right!" said Lee Literal. "It is I, the superhero who takes everything literally."

"Tear him limb from limb!" shouted the Exaggerator.

Lee Literal proceeded to tear Mr. Idiom's arms and legs off.

"Oooh, that's gotta hurt!" yelled Captain Obvious.

"Kick his butt!" shouted the Exaggerator.

Lee Literal proceeded to kick Mr. Idiom's butt.

"Punch his lights out!" shouted the Exaggerator.

"What lights?" asked Lee Literal. "He doesn't have any lights."

"Forget it," Captain Obvious said. "He's not breathing, and he has no pulse. I think he's dead."

"The big bad bum bled big bad blood badly," I said.

"As always, we have conquered the forces of evil," said Captain Obvious, high-fiving the Exaggerator.

"We couldn't have done it without your help, Alliterator," the Exaggerator told me.

"How much dew would a dewdrop drop, if a dewdrop did drop dew?" I asked.

"That doesn't make any sense," said Captain Obvious.

"Are you suggesting that anything up till now has made sense?" asked the Exaggerator.

It had been a long day. Twenty-four hours long, to be exact. I was glad it was over. All of those silly characters were just so annoying to be around.

"Well, our work here is done," said Captain Obvious.

"After all that excitement, I need to blow off some steam," said Lee Literal.

So we went inside Mr. Idiom's house and put a teapot on the stove. When steam started coming out of it, Lee Literal blew it off.

"What now?" I asked.

"Before we part company, let's say inappropriate and immature words," Captain Obvious suggested.

"Why?" I asked.

"Because they're funny!" said Captain Obvious.

So we proceeded to say the most inappropriate and immature words we could think of.

"Fart."

"Doody-face."

"Boogers and snot."

Chapter 7

Mystery

Who Was the Killer of Principal Miller?

"Boogers and snot," said my friend Lionel, "would be a good name for a rock band."

"Yeah," I said, "like Guns N' Roses."

I was at school, in the hallway outside the main office. Kids and teachers were rushing around. It must be before first period. There was a sign on the door with an arrow pointing to the media center: THERE'S NO PLACE LIKE A BOOK FAIR! I was wearing my backpack. Everything looked so . . . normal! I pinched myself to see if I was dreaming. It hurt.

What a relief! I could go back to my normal life. At last.

And then suddenly . . .

"Eeeeeeeeeeeeeeekkkkkkkkkkkk!"

Our school secretary, Mrs. Conners, came running out of the office.

"It's Principal Miller!" she shouted. "He's . . . dead!"

Panic. There was yelling and running and sobbing. Cell phones appeared instantly and everybody was dialing 911. The nurse, Mrs. Robinson, came running over from her office with a first aid kit. The vice principal, Mrs. DeLuca, came running out of her office.

It seemed as if only a few seconds had passed before sirens were screaming down the street and cars screeched to a halt outside school. Cops came running in with their guns drawn. Detectives. Emergency medical teams. It was pandemonium.

A lot of kids headed for the exits, but Lionel and I stuck around to see what would happen next. Principal Miller had been a great guy. All the kids had loved him. He had won the Principal of the Year award a few years back. You'd always see him around town at sporting events and charity functions. It was hard to believe anyone would kill him. We waited patiently in the hall for a long time, until finally one of the policemen came out of the office and told us he had an announcement.

"My name is Officer Joseph Bolton," he said. "Principal Miller is deceased. The cause of death was heart failure, brought on by intense electrical stimulation. We have examined all the clues and evidence. There is one person of interest we need to question immediately. It is crucial that we find a young man named . . ."

He pulled a piece of paper out of his pocket and read it.

". . . Trip Dinkleman."

What????!!!!

Everybody gasped and turned to look at me.

"Dink didn't do anything!" Lionel shouted.

"I'm Trip Dinkleman," I said. "Why do you need to question *me*?"

Officer Bolton looked me up and down slowly.

"Why don't you just tell the truth, Dinkleman?" he said. "You can make it easy on all of us."

"The truth is I was at the book fair and some books fell on my head," I explained, "and the next thing I knew I was at some haunted house where some guy tried to give me a face transplant. And then I was at the Super Bowl. And then—"

"The kid is an obvious liar," Officer Bolton said. "Let me see his backpack, boys."

A couple of cops came over. I willingly handed over my backpack.

"Go ahead and check it," I told them. "I have nothing to hide."

The two cops brought my backpack over to Officer Bolton. He unzipped the larger pocket and reached inside.

"Well, maybe you should have hidden *this*," he

said, as he pulled out a small black device that was about the size of a deck of cards.

"What's that?" I asked. "I've never seen that before."

"You know perfectly well what it is, Mr. Dinkleman," said Officer Bolton. "It's a stun gun!"

Everybody gasped, including me. I felt a hundred pairs of eyes peering into my soul.

"What's the deal, Dink?" Lionel asked.

"Miller had a weak heart," Officer Bolton said. "Fifty thousand volts was more than enough to stop it."

"Trip! How *could* you?" Vice Principal DeLuca said. "You were always such a nice boy!"

"How could I do *what*?" I protested.

"You killed Principal Miller!" said Mrs. Conners, and she broke down crying.

"I did not!" I shouted. "I didn't put that in my backpack."

"Tell it to the judge, kid," said Officer Bolton.

I didn't know what to do. How did that stun gun get into my backpack? There was no time to think things over. I could stay there and argue my case, but it wasn't looking good. Everyone was staring at me with venom in their eyes. Even Lionel.

I made a snap decision. I bolted out of there. I yanked open the stairwell door and dashed down to the ground floor. The front door to the school was open, and I jumped down the front steps. I don't think my feet ever touched the ground.

They would be coming after me: that was for sure. I had never run so fast in my life. I peeked behind me quickly. The cops weren't there yet.

Going home was out of the question. That would be the first place the cops would look. I headed downtown, down to the sleazier part of town.

I was out of breath, but I couldn't stop running. Not yet. There had to be a place to hide until I could collect my thoughts. People on the street glanced at me as I ran past, but nobody tried to stop me. In this part of town, it's not unusual to see people running from the law.

The street was filled with bars, pawnshops, and low-rent beauty parlors. I had to find a place soon or I'd collapse. Then I saw a sign: JAMES SNARK, PRIVATE EYE. I ducked in the doorway and slammed the door behind me.

"Don't you know how to knock?" somebody muttered. I turned around to see who said it.

Leaning back in a battered leather chair was a guy wearing one of those old-time felt hats with a brim. His feet were up on an old wooden desk. There was a cigarette dangling from his lips.

"Are you James Snark?" I asked, panting between words.

"That's what it says on the alimony checks," he replied.

"You've gotta help me, Mr. Snark! The police are after me!"

"Calm down," he said. "Take a load off. You're safe here. The cops are afraid to come into this neighborhood."

I told him the whole story of what had happened to me at school. He grabbed a pad out of his desk drawer and started scribbling notes. When I was finished, he let out a whistle.

"Lemme make one thing clear, kid," he said. "I charge top dollar for my services. This is gonna cost you a pretty penny."

"My parents will pay," I told him. "I can call them—"

He slammed his hand down on the phone before I could pick up the receiver.

"The cops are at your house right now," he said. "Bet on it. You say you didn't kill Principal Miller. Is that the truth, or are you lying to me?"

"It's the truth," I said. "I swear it."

"Well, *somebody's* lying," Snark said. "That somebody must've zapped Miller and planted the

stun gun in your backpack. Do you have any enemies?"

"Not that I know of."

"What about that kid Lionel?"

"He's my best friend," I said. "He would never
do that." I decided not to mention that Lionel had
pushed me out of a plane once.

"How about Principal Miller?" Snark asked.
"Did anybody hate him?"

"Gee, I don't know," I said. "I always liked him."

"Huh, and you're the one they're trying to pin
his murder on. Life is funny that way. I'm gonna
have to do a little snooping around."

Snark got up and put his coat on.

"If I can't go home, where should I go?" I asked.

"You can cool your heels upstairs in my place
until the heat's off," he told me. "There are some
Pop-Tarts in the fridge."

"I don't suppose you have any funnel cake?" I
asked.

"Funnel cake?"

"Never mind," I said. "I can't thank you enough, Mr. Snark."

"Just doing my job, kid," he said, slamming the door behind him.

Snark here. I spent the next few weeks snooping around on behalf of the Dinkleman kid, seeing what dirt I could dig up on the Miller murder. And believe me, I dug up a lot. Turns out sweet old Principal Miller wasn't such a pillar of the community after all. He was a rotten principal, a rotten husband, a rotten father, and a rotten man. He had more than a few enemies and lots of skeletons in his closet, not to mention some really ugly ties. In fact, just about everybody hated him. It was only a matter of time before somebody decided to off him.

After I finished my investigation, I called all the interested parties into my office, including the

Dinkleman kid. The murder had been all over the papers, and there had been a nationwide manhunt for Dinkleman, but nobody had thought to look in my guest room. I invited Officer Joseph Bolton and Miller's widow to the big pow-wow too.

This is how it went down . . .

"Ladies and gentleman," I said, once they got over the shock of seeing Dinkleman sitting there alive and well, "my name is James Snark, and I'm a private investigator. I called you all here to discuss the stun-gun murder of Principal Horace Miller on April 18."

A few of them started sobbing, but I didn't break stride. Sometimes it's my job to make people cry.

"Are you suggesting that one of us is a suspect?" asked Sharon DeLuca, the vice principal at Miller's school.

"No, sweetheart," I told her. "I'm suggesting that *all* of you are suspects. All of you had a motive to kill Principal Miller. I know exactly who did it, and I'm going to name names."

"That's ridiculous!" Mrs. DeLuca replied.

"Maybe yes, maybe no," I said. "Would you mind if I asked you a few questions, Mrs. DeLuca?"

"Ask away," she said. "I'll take a lie detector test if you want."

"Did you kill Principal Miller?" I asked directly. No point beating around the bush.

"Of course not!" she said, looking as guilty as sin to me.

"Mrs. DeLuca," I said politely, "two years ago, when the previous principal retired, you were next in line to be principal, weren't you?"

"I suppose so," she replied.

"You would have gotten a nice raise in salary if you had been promoted to principal. But they hired Horace Miller from another school instead."

"Your point?" she asked.

"You wanted that principal's job, didn't you?" I asked.

"I made no secret about that."

"MAYBE YOU WANTED IT BADLY ENOUGH TO KILL HIM!" I shouted, spitting the words in her direction.

"That's preposterous!" she exclaimed, flustered.

"Maybe it is, and maybe it isn't," I said. I had a few more questions to ask her, but there were other fish I wanted to fry first.

I turned my attention to the president of the PTA, a Mrs. Jennifer Pontoon.

"Mrs. Pontoon," I said, "last fall you were planning to hold a fund-raiser to buy the school one of those computerized whiteboards, weren't you?"

"Yes, I was," she replied.

"But Principal Miller wouldn't let you sell gift wrap to raise money, is that correct?"

"Yes, so what?" she blabbered.

"How did that make you feel?" I asked.

"Upset," Mrs. Pontoon admitted. "A little angry."

"ANGRY ENOUGH TO KILL HIM?" I asked.

"I would never kill *anybody*!" she said, her voice cracking. "I'm with the PTA!"

"Um-hmmm," I muttered. "What about you, Mrs. Robinson? You're the school nurse. Is it true that you have access to a number of toxic chemicals—shall we say poisons—in the nurse's office?"

"Certainly," she replied. "I have a lot of medicine, and some of it can be toxic if taken in large doses."

"DO YOU HAVE ENOUGH TO KILL A MAN?" I asked. "Or should I say, *did* you have enough before you killed Principal Miller?"

"The principal had a heart attack!" she yelled at me, her eyes fiery. "You said somebody caused it with a stun gun!"

"What if I were to tell you," I said, "that the autopsy revealed a large quantity of ibuprofen in Principal Miller's body?"

"I'd say that he must have had a headache," she replied.

"A HEADACHE BAD ENOUGH TO KILL HIM?" I asked.

"I didn't do it!" she yelled at me. But I ignored her and turned my attention to the school secretary.

"Mrs. Conners, can you tell us what a school secretary does?"

"I make announcements, sort the mail, keep track of which students are absent, things like that," Mrs. Conners said.

"But Principal Miller made you do other things too, didn't he?" I asked. "He made you buy a gift for his wife when he forgot their anniversary. He made you give his dog a haircut. He made you wash his car, isn't that right?"

"Yes, so what?" she said.

"You have a master's degree in business, don't you, Mrs. Conners?" I asked her. "You worked hard to earn that degree, didn't you?"

"Yes, I did," she replied.

"Tell me, Mrs. Conners. Does a person with a master's degree like or dislike giving haircuts to a dog?"

She squirmed in her seat.

"I disliked it," she admitted.

"DID YOU DISLIKE IT ENOUGH TO KILL HIM?"

I didn't even give her the chance to answer. I swiveled my chair around until I was facing the school custodian, a guy named Herb Dunn.

"Mr. Dunn, you didn't like Principal Miller very much, did you?"

"Lots of people hated him," Dunn said in broken English.

"Just answer the question," I said, sighing. "Yes or no?"

"No, I didn't like him," said Dunn.

"He didn't give you enough time to mop the floor of the cafeteria and let it dry before the kids

came in for afternoon assemblies, isn't that right?"
I asked.

"That's right."

"Were there any other things he did that bothered you?" I asked.

"Sure, lots of things," Mr. Dunn said.

"ENOUGH THINGS THAT YOU'D WANT TO KILL HIM?"

I turned my attention to the science teacher, Mr. Reggie Chan.

"Mr. Chan, where were you on the morning of April 18?" I asked.

"I was in the science room, as always," Chan replied.

"What if I told you that surveillance video shows the science room was empty at the moment when Principal Miller was murdered?" I said.

"Perhaps I stepped out briefly," Chan said.

"Yes, I guess you had a little time . . . TO KILL!"

They were sweating now, all of them. Nobody was saying anything about arresting the Dinkleman kid anymore. Any one of them could have zapped Principal Miller and stashed the stun gun in Dinkleman's backpack. They all had motives and they all looked guilty. I turned to the school media specialist, Miss Rosemary Durkin.

"You have a difficult job, don't you, Miss Durkin?"

"We all do," she replied.

"But we all don't have to be the librarian at two schools a mile apart," I pointed out. "We all didn't have Principal Miller take away our assistant due to budget cuts last year. We all don't have to teach eight classes a day, every day. We all don't have to shelve books by ourselves. We all don't have to do story time with whining first graders. Isn't it true that you barely have time to go to the bathroom during the day? Isn't it true that nobody ever thanks you for all you do at school? Isn't it true that when you get home at the end of the day, you're so tired you eat frozen dinners without even heating them up?"

"Yes, it's true!" she complained. "So what?"

"And isn't it true that one day in the teacher's lounge you said you wished Principal Miller would drop dead?" I asked.

"I was joking!" she protested.

"DO YOU THINK MURDER IS A JOKE, MISS DURKIN?"

She pulled a handkerchief out of her pocket and dabbed her eyes with it. Three or four of them were crying by now, including Mrs. Sylvia Miller, the widow of Principal Miller. And she just happened to be the next person I wanted to question.

"How long were you and Principal Miller married?" I asked her gently.

"Twenty years," she said, sobbing.

"That's a long time," I said. "Was it a good marriage?"

"Yes. Are you suggesting that I murdered my husband?" asked Mrs. Miller.

"I didn't say that," I told her. "I'm just curious why, on the night of April 17, you were seen on surveillance video at the Acropolis Diner playing footsie under the table with . . . Officer Joseph Bolton!"

Everybody around the table gasped. All heads turned to look at Officer Bolton.

"Don't drag *me* into this, Snark!" he shouted, pointing a finger at my face. "My relationship with Mrs. Miller is purely professional."

"Oh yeah?" I said. "Tell me this, Officer Bolton. How did you know the stun gun was in Trip Dinkleman's backpack? There was no metal detector at the school. The only way you could have known the stun gun was there was if you put it there yourself!"

"That's a lie!" Officer Bolton hollered.

"Admit it, *you* put the stun gun in the backpack

to frame Dinkleman!" I said, getting out of my seat to confront him. "Yes, and *you* made sure to pull it out of that backpack personally so there would be a reason for your fingerprints being on it! And *you* zapped Miller so you and his wife would be free to get married! Admit it!"

"It's true! It's true!" Sylvia Miller shouted, before breaking down in tears. "We killed Horace! I can't take the guilt any longer!"

"Case closed," I said.

Wow! Mr. Snark put on an awesome performance. When it was all over, he shook my hand and everybody came over to hug me. Well, everyone except for Mrs. Miller and Officer Joseph Bolton, who were taken away by the police.

"How can I ever thank you?" I asked James Snark.

"Don't thank me, kid," he said, handing me an envelope. "I'm just doing my job."

I opened the envelope. It was Snark's bill. I looked down at the bottom for the total. There was a zero. And another zero. And another zero. And another zero. I felt as if I was going to pass out.

Intermission I

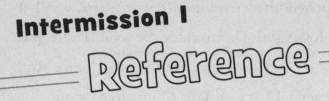

Find the Secret Hidden Message!

A

ad-o-les-cent Growing to adulthood, youthful. A person in the period of adolescence.

B

boy A male child, from birth to full growth. A young man. A son. Sometimes found at a book fair.

C

cap-tive A prisoner. A person who is enslaved or dominated. Made or held prisoner. Kept in confinement.

I may possibly be in a . . .

co-ma A state of prolonged unconsciousness, including a lack of response to stimuli, from which it is impossible to rouse a person.

Or maybe I'm just having a . . .

D
dream A succession of images, thoughts, or emotions passing through the mind during sleep. An involuntary vision occurring to a person when awake.

I dreamed I was . . .

E
eat-ing The act of taking food into the mouth and swallowing it for nourishment. Chewing and swallowing.

F
fun-nel cake Deliciously sweet specialty food, originally associated with the Pennsylvania Dutch region, that is popular at ballparks, fairs, and festivals.

G

get To go after, take hold of, and bring (something) for oneself or another. To cause or cause to become, to do, to move. To communicate or establish communication with over a distance.

H

help To save, rescue. To relieve someone in need, sickness, pain, or distress. To give aid, to be of service or advantage. To assist, as during a time of need.

I

I The nominative singular pronoun used by a speaker or writer in referring to himself or herself. Used to denote the narrator of a literary work written in the first person singular.

J

just Exactly or precisely. Only or merely. Simply.

K

keep To continue in a given position, state, course, or action. To maintain in condition or order.

L

liv-ing Having life, being alive. Active or thriving, vigorous, strong. The act or condition of a person or a thing that lives.

M

my The nominative singular possessive pronoun, used by a speaker in referring to himself or herself.

N

night-mare A terrifying dream producing feelings of extreme fear and anxiety. A monster or evil spirit believed to oppress persons during sleep.

O

o-ver and o-ver Many times, repeatedly.

P

please Used as a polite addition to requests, commands, etc. If you would be so obliging, kindly. The magic word.

Q

quick-ly With speed, rapidly, very soon.

R

res-cue To free from confinement or danger.

S

sleep-ing The suspension of voluntary bodily functions and the natural suspension, complete or partial, of consciousness. Unawake.

stu-dent A person formally engaged in learning.

T

ter-ri-fied Filled with terror or alarm, made greatly afraid.

trapped Caught unaware by a mechanical device, stratagem, or trick. Forced into an unpleasant or confining situation from which it is difficult to escape.

By...

U

u-biq-ui-tous Existing or being everywhere, especially at the same time.

ug-ly Very unattractive or displeasing in appearance.

un-bal-anced Mentally disordered, disturbed, or deranged.

un-bear-a-ble Unendurable, intolerable.

un-friend-ly Not kind, unsympathetic, aloof, hostile, antagonistic.

u-nique Having no like or equal, incomparable, not typical, unusual.

un-pleas-ant Displeasing, disagreeable, offensive.

un-pre-dict-a-ble Variable, uncertain, erratic.

un-re-lent-ing Not easing or slackening, as in intensity, speed, or vigor.

un-sta-ble Liable to change or fluctuate quickly, marked by emotional instability.

un-u-su-al Not usual or ordinary, uncommon.

V

vi-cious Immoral or evil, depraved, spiteful, malicious, savage, ferocious, unruly, fierce.

vi-o-lent Acting with uncontrolled destructive force.

W

weird-os Odd, eccentric, or abnormal people.

X

XOXOXOXOX Hugs and kisses.

Y

yours tru-ly Closing of letter, term of endearment.

Z

ZZZZZZZZzzzzzzzzzz

Chapter 8
Historical Fiction

Houston, We Have a Problem

ZZZZZZZZZzzzzzzzzzz.

I opened my eyes. I was staring out a small triangular window. There was a planet out there. It looked like a big blue marble floating in the blackness of outer space. Hmmm, that was odd.

I turned around. There were three guys staring at me. Two of them had blond hair. I screamed.

"Who are you?!" I yelled.

"Who are *you*?" all three of them yelled right back. One of them rushed to grab a microphone.

"Houston, we have a problem!" the guy with dark hair shouted.

"My name is Trip Dinkleman," I told them. "I

was at this book fair, and I just wanted to get to lacrosse tryouts, and something fell on my head, and—"

"No time for that!" snapped the dark-haired one. It said COLLINS on the blue uniform he was wearing. "How did you get in here?"

"I don't know," I said truthfully. "A couple of minutes ago I was fighting crime with these strange superheroes. And then I was accused of murdering my principal. Weird things keep happening to me."

"This is Mission Control in Houston," said a voice from a speaker. "What is the problem, Columbia? Over."

The three of them looked at each other. Collins turned off the microphone.

"Do you have any idea where you are, kid?" asked one of the two blond guys. It said ALDRIN on his uniform.

I looked around. It was a room about the size of

a minivan with five very small windows and stuff all over the place. There was an instrument panel with hundreds of knobs and switches. I looked out the window at the planet again.

"On a spaceship?" I guessed.

"This is *Apollo 11*," said the other blond guy. He had a patch on his uniform that said ARMSTRONG. "We're on our way to the moon."

"Repeat," said the voice in the speaker. "What is the problem, Columbia? Over."

"I'm sorry!" I told the three guys. "I didn't mean for this to happen. I just want to go home."

"Kids don't just appear out of nowhere," Aldrin said.

"If Houston finds out about this, they'll abort the mission," Collins told the others.

"Aborting at this point would be just as risky as continuing the mission," Aldrin said.

"We've trained our whole lives for this," said

Armstrong. "We're not turning back now because some kid stowed away on our ship. We might as well make the best of it."

All three agreed.

"Not one word of this to *anyone*," Armstrong told me, locking eyes with mine. "You understand?"

"Anything you say," I replied.

Collins turned the mic back on.

"No problem, Houston," he said. "It was a false alarm."

I knew the name Neil Armstrong. Everybody knows that Neil Armstrong was the first person to set foot on the moon. It's one of those things you just know, like the fact that George Washington was the first president and Thomas Edison invented the lightbulb. But here I was, two feet away from the man.

The other two guys I didn't know. But Aldrin told me to call him Buzz, Collins told me to call him

Mike, and Armstrong told me to call him Neil. He seemed to be the one in charge. He looked like the kind of guy who couldn't be rattled by anything.

Once we had gotten over the initial shock of seeing each other, they told me it was July 16, 1969. With the help of seven and a half million pounds of thrust, they had already lifted off from Cape Kennedy in Florida. Several stages of their Saturn 5 rocket had been burned off to get them into orbit around the earth.

In order to break away from the earth's gravity, a spaceship has to be moving 24,000 miles an hour, Neil explained to me. They fired their engines to do that just before I showed up. From that point, it's almost 240,000 miles to the moon.

Don't ask me how I ended up in a spaceship going to the moon. Don't ask me how I ended up in 1969. I have no idea. And I wasn't about to tell them I was from the twenty-first century. They'd think I was crazy.

I looked at the earth through the triangular window again. It was slightly smaller than it was the first time. We were moving away from it. I could see the huge blue oceans. Swirling white clouds covered much of the planet, which made it hard to pick out specific countries or continents. I thought I could see the outline of Florida, but I wasn't sure. It was a beautiful sight.

Out the window on the other side of the ship, I could see the the moon. It had never occurred to me how complicated it might be to send a spaceship there. But Buzz made it clearer.

"You ever play football, Trip?" he asked.

"Yeah, sure," I said, recalling my brief Super Bowl experience.

"Then you know what it's like to complete a pass," he said. "The quarterback doesn't throw the ball to the receiver. He throws it to where the receiver is going to *be* at a certain point in time. That's what we're trying to do with the moon."

Buzz explained that what they were trying to do was even harder than completing a pass. Because not only were they trying to hit a moving target, but the earth spins and revolves around the sun, and the moon spins and revolves around the earth. Plus, the moon is only about a quarter of the size of the earth. So the timing of everything has to be perfect.

An incomplete pass would mean three guys were going to die. Well, three guys and me, now.

As Buzz was talking, I felt a strange sensation. It was almost as if I was losing weight. And I was. The farther we got from the earth, the less we were affected by the earth's gravity. And then, quite suddenly, I felt myself float off the floor.

We were weightless. The four of us lifted up simultaneously, and even though the three of them had all experienced weightlessness before, smiles spread across their faces. It was irresistible, like tasting ice cream for the first time.

There wasn't a lot of room in there. I bumped

into Neil and Neil bumped into Mike, sending him floating off to the other end of the ship. I pushed off the wall and tucked my legs in so I could spin around and do a somersault in the air. There was no up or down anymore. You just keep turning until you bump into something.

I could have fooled around like that for hours, but the others had work to do. They began to check all the equipment and systems, conduct scientific experiments, and they even made a short TV show so the people back home on earth could see what they were up to. They were careful to keep me out of it, of course. There would be a lot of explaining to do if some kid showed up in the pictures. It was cool watching them work while weightless, floating the tools and equipment back and forth.

Outside the little windows, space was getting darker and darker as we got farther from the earth's atmosphere. It was blacker than any black I had ever seen.

"Commence barbecue roll," Neil ordered.

"What's that?" I asked.

Mike told me that the heat from the sun could fry the fuel tanks and cause a nasty explosion if we stayed in one position. So they did a barbecue roll—a slow roll that heated all sides of the ship evenly. It was kind of like a chicken roasting in a rotisserie oven.

"This is making me hungry," Mike said. "What do you say we eat?"

Buzz opened up a door and pulled out some aluminum bags, which floated across the cabin. He grabbed one and also grabbed a scissors to cut the tip of the bag off. Then he took a thing off the wall that looked like a little water gun.

"What's that?" I asked.

"A water gun," Mike said. It was a *hot* water gun, to be more specific. Mike pulled the trigger and squirted some water into the bag. A half an ounce for each squeeze. All the food had to be in a bag because if you just put it on a plate or in a cup, the food would float away. They told me that they carried just a little water on the ship, but they also had a fuel cell that took hydrogen and oxygen and combined them to produce water.

"What are you making?" I asked.

"Corn chowder," Buzz said.

"Here," he said, handing me the bag. "Try it."

I put the tip of the bag to my lips and suddenly panicked.

"What if the food gets caught in my throat?" I asked. "Doesn't it need gravity to push it down?"

They all laughed, so I figured there was nothing to worry about. I squeezed the bag and the corn chowder squirted into my mouth. Not bad! I swallowed it easily and passed the bag around to the others.

I read the labels on the other bags that were floating around the cabin. Chicken salad. Applesauce. Shrimp cocktail. Sugar cookies. Orange drink. We were going to have a feast!

"Slow down, cowboy!" Neil said. "This has got to last us six days."

Oh. Well, it wasn't exactly a feast, but it was just as good as most of my school lunches, I'll say that much.

I had no idea what time it was, and you couldn't tell by looking out the window, that was for sure. Outside, it was night *all* the time. Anyway, I was sleepy, and I wasn't the only one. The others shaded the windows, dimmed the lights, and pulled out three sleeping bags. Neil was nice enough to let me use his, and he tied one end to a pole so I wouldn't float all over the place and bump into things.

I was tired, but too excited to sleep, I guess. Even if this whole thing was a hallucination, I was hallucinating about going to the moon! It was way better than hallucinating that you're in a haunted house or trapped in a dictionary.

While we lay there with the lights out, they told

me a little bit about themselves. Neil and Buzz were Navy fighter pilots. Between the two of them, they had flown 144 combat missions in the Korean War. Mike was an air force test pilot. When the space program began, a bunch of those guys joined up. The three of them were the lucky ones who were chosen to go to the moon.

"I still remember President Kennedy's exact words in May of 1961," Neil said. "'I believe this nation should commit itself to achieve the goal, before this decade is out, of landing a man on the moon and returning him safely to earth.'"

"And here we are," said Buzz, "five months early."

Before the Apollo program, they told me, NASA had the Mercury and Gemini programs. In Mercury, astronauts orbited the earth and got the hang of living and working in space. In Gemini, they practiced docking two ships together. In Apollo, astronauts went all the way to the moon and orbited it. Finally, they were ready to attempt a landing.

The interesting thing is that the whole time, the Russians were racing to do the same thing. In fact, just two weeks before Neil, Buzz, and Mike lifted off, the Russians launched an unmanned ship they hoped to land on the moon and bring back some moon rocks before we did.

"Why is being first so important?" I asked. "Who cares who gets there first?"

"It's symbolic," Neil said. "Whoever gets to the moon first essentially wins the Cold War."

I didn't tell them what I had learned in social studies—that we *were* going to win The Cold War. The Soviet Union was going to collapse in 1991. Who knows? Maybe the fact that we got to the moon first was one of the reasons the Soviet Union collapsed.

Neil, Buzz, and Mike had stopped talking. Maybe they were asleep. I was afraid that if I went to sleep, it would all be over. I would wake up in some completely different place, a completely different strange situation. For a change, I didn't want to go home. I wanted to go to the moon.

"Which one of you gets to step on the moon first?" I whispered, knowing the answer full well.

"Me," Neil said.

"What are you going to say?" I asked. I also knew what he was going to say. Everybody knows what he said.

"I have no idea. I haven't even thought about it."

"You should say something significant," I suggested. "The whole world will be watching."

"You're right."

"Hey, I'll bet if you said something like 'eat at McDonald's' or 'Drink Pepsi,' they would pay you a million dollars."

Neil chuckled quietly. Then I said good night, but he didn't answer, and I heard snoring so I guess he had gone to sleep.

❀ ❀ ❀

I don't know how long I was out, but it must have been a while. When I opened my eyes and looked out the window, the earth was much smaller. Out the other window, the moon was *huge*. It was whitish gray, with millions of craters all over the place. Some looked like volcanoes, while others looked like meteors had crashed into them. We were getting close.

Neil, Buzz, and Mike were bustling about, doing chores and experiments. They helped me out of the sleeping bag and gave me some cream of chicken soup to eat.

"You guys don't have any funnel cake, do you?" I asked.

"No, why?" Buzz replied.

"Just wondering. Say, what if you're on the moon and a meteor hits you?" I asked Neil.

"I guess we would become a crater," he replied.

Mostly, I kept out of their way. There wasn't

much for me to do, and the three of them were busy. I didn't want to interfere. But I wondered what they had in mind for me once they got to the moon. I knew that Mike was going to stay in the command module orbiting the moon while Neil and Buzz went to the surface in a smaller part of the ship called the lunar excursion module or LEM. But what about me?

Gradually, I began to notice that something felt different. My body felt heavier. Maybe I had eaten too much. But then the stuff that was floating around the cabin started settling to the floor.

"It's the moon's gravity," Buzz told me. "It's starting to pull us in."

I didn't even know the moon *had* gravity.

We were 38,000 miles away, Mike announced. I could sense that the three of them were getting excited. Our velocity had increased to 5,512 feet per second. But I had no sense of speed. It's not like when you're in a car and you see trees and houses and street signs whizzing past. There was nothing outside.

I spent a lot of time looking out the window at the moon. It was sometimes gray and sometimes brown, depending on how the sun's rays were striking it.

Neil, Buzz, and Mike went over and strapped themselves into their seats, with serious looks on their faces.

"Prepare for engine burn," Neil said.

They had told me they would have to fire the main rockets to slow the ship down so it would be captured by the moon's gravity. Like everything else, it had to be done at the exactly correct moment.

"If the engine doesn't fire for some reason, we'll loop around the moon and come back to earth," Buzz said.

"What if you fire it too long?" I asked.

"We crash into the moon," he replied.

It was really tense for a few minutes, and then

I felt the thrust of the engine jolting us into orbit around the moon. There was a general sense of relief in the cabin. Things must have gone according to plan.

We would be out of touch with Mission Control for thirty-three minutes as we swung around because the radio signals could not bend around the moon.

"*Apollo 11*, this is Houston," the radio crackled, as soon as we popped out the other side. "How do you read? Could you repeat your burn status-report?"

"Reading you loud and clear, Houston," Neil said. "It was like . . . perfect."

We woke up the next morning, Sunday, July 20—to a lunar sunrise. First there was a thin white haze over the horizon, and then the sun blasted into view. It was a sight I'll never forget. We ate breakfast (freeze-dried eggs, yum!), and Neil opened a closet and took out a bulky white space suit. It was the kind with the big helmet I had seen in pictures.

"It's time," he said to Buzz.

Neil and Buzz each climbed into their suits, and Mike helped them with the latches, oxygen hoses, and life-support backpacks.

"Good luck," I said, a little disappointed that I wouldn't be joining them.

"Good luck, nothing," Neil said. "Trip, you're coming with us."

"You mean it?!" I asked.

"We might need your help down there," Buzz said.

They had a third suit as a backup, and Mike helped me into it. It was a little big on me, but not too bad. Once I was all zipped up, Mike wrapped his arms around the three of us. He didn't say a word, but I knew what he meant when I looked into his eyes. If anything went wrong—and a lot of things could go wrong—we would never see him again. We would never see *anybody* again.

There was a tunnel at one end of the command module. Neil opened the hatch and the three of us crawled through the tunnel into the lunar module, which they called *Eagle*. It wasn't easy. Our suits were bulky, and the tunnel was barely wide enough to squeeze through. But eventually we made it. Buzz sealed the hatch that separated the command module from the lunar module.

The *Eagle* was sort of an ugly thing that looked a little bit like a spider, with exposed wires and pipes. It wasn't streamlined as you would expect a spaceship to be. Buzz told me it didn't need to be streamlined because the moon has no atmosphere to slow it down.

They sat in front of the big instrument panel, which even had a gauge to indicate Neil's heart rate. It was steady at seventy-seven beats per minute.

We were orbiting about sixty miles above the

moon. During the thirteenth orbit, a voice from Houston crackled over the radio.

"You are go for separation, Columbia."

Neil pushed a button, and I felt a bump. The *Eagle* had separated from Mike's command module. Out the window, I could see the command module drifting a few yards away. We were floating, if you can call moving at 3,700 miles per hour floating. Neil's heart rate had jumped to eighty-five beats per minute.

"Fire descent rocket," Buzz said, and suddenly we were moving away from the command module and toward the surface of the moon.

"How does it look?" radioed Mission Control.

"The *Eagle* has wings," Neil replied. "The burn was on time." His heart rate was at ninety-six.

"Listen, baby," Mike's voice said over the radio, "things are going just swimmingly, just beautiful."

Neil's heart rate jumped to 110. He had to pilot the *Eagle* 300 miles across the moon, dropping down in a long curve from 50,000 feet. We were upside down. I couldn't see the moon.

Green lights blinked the number 99 on the computer display. That meant Neil had five seconds to decide if he wanted to go ahead and attempt a landing or return to the command module. His heart rate was 125. He pressed the PROCEED button.

"*Eagle*, Houston," said a voice in the speaker. "You are go to continue power descent."

"Twenty-one thousand feet," Buzz told Neil. We were going fast now.

"Fifteen thousand . . . ten thousand . . . seventy-two hundred feet," Buzz reported. "Landing site five miles ahead."

We were going to land on a part of the moon called the Sea of Tranquillity. It had been mapped out from photos taken on previous unmanned flights, and it was chosen because the surface was smooth.

We were slowing down. Neil was at the controls,

but a computer was controlling the landing at this point. It automatically turned *Eagle* upside down into landing position. I could see the surface of the moon now. There were hills, ridges, and lots of craters.

We were dropping twenty feet per second. Neil's heart rate was 135.

How did they know the moon's surface was solid, I wondered. What if it was like deep snow, and the *Eagle* would just sink into it? I guessed that previous missions had shown that wouldn't happen. I didn't want to bother them with questions. Not now.

We were five hundred feet over the surface of the moon, directly over the landing site.

"Not good!" Neil suddenly said urgently, shaking his head. His heart rate was 147.

"Large crater," Buzz said, "about the size of a football field. Filled with boulders and rocks."

They didn't have to explain it to me. If we landed on a steep tilt or on one of those boulders, we might tip over. Even if we didn't tip over, we would be pointing at the wrong angle when it was time to blast off the moon. Either way, we would die.

Neil flipped a switch and grabbed the joystick.

"I'm going to look for another parking spot," he announced.

"Ninety seconds, *Eagle*," said Mission Control.

That meant we had ninety seconds' worth of fuel. The lunar module couldn't carry a lot of fuel, and most of it had to be saved so we could lift off from the moon later.

Neil pulled back on the stick and we skimmed over the big crater of rocks. He and Buzz were looking quickly left and right at the surface of the moon for a smooth area to land. So was I.

"Sixty seconds," Mission Control said.

"Lights on," Neil said, and the surface brightened up immediately.

"Over there!" Neil said, pushing the stick.

"Forward. Good," Buzz said. "Forty feet, down two and a half."

"Picking up some dust," Neil said. "Thirty feet, two and a half down. Faint shadow. Four forward. Four forward. Drifting to the right a little."

"Dead man's zone," Buzz said.

If we ran out of fuel here, we would be finished. We were four miles west of the target. Neil's heart rate was 156.

"Thirty seconds," Mission Control announced.

We were right over the moon. I could have jumped out the window at this height and landed on my feet. A blue light flashed. We were kicking up dust. There was a bump.

"Contact light," Buzz said.

"Okay, engine stop," said Neil. "Houston, Tranquillity Base here. The *Eagle* has landed."

For the first time in history, human beings had landed on the moon.

And I was one of them.

❁ ❁ ❁

The dust settled and I could see the surface. There were hills in the distance, maybe twenty or thirty feet high. Shallow craters, about the size of manhole covers, were all over the place. Some bigger. Looking up, I could see the earth. So far away.

I was anxious to get out and walk on the moon, but Neil and Buzz had things to do first. They checked over the *Eagle* to make sure it hadn't been damaged by the landing. We had some food—bacon squares, sugar cookies, peaches, juice, and coffee. Finally, Buzz and I snapped on Neil's helmet and strapped one of the life-support systems to his back. Buzz cautioned me to be careful. If something ripped or there was a tiny hole anywhere, Neil would suffocate instantly.

Neil opened the hatch and attached a TV camera to one of *Eagle*'s legs. Then he made the slow descent down the ladder. I watched out the window and could hear Neil's words through the microphone in his helmet.

"I'm at the foot of the ladder," he said. "The footpads are only depressed in the surface about one or two inches, although the surface appears to be very fine-grained as you get close to it. I'm going to step off the LEM now."

There was no sound for a moment. It was so quiet. I couldn't hear anything except for my own heartbeat. The sky was filled with stars, and it was a little strange because when you're on the moon, they don't twinkle. I had never really noticed that stars twinkle before. I guess it's the earth's atmosphere that makes them do that.

Neil put his left foot on the moon, and then he said the words I was waiting for. It would take exactly 1.3 seconds before the signal would reach billions of ears on earth.

"That's one small step for man, one giant leap for mankind."

DAN GUTMAN

"Good line," Buzz said.

"The surface is fine and powdery," Neil continued, once both of his feet were on the moon. "I can pick it up loosely with my toe."

When Neil gave us the go-ahead, Buzz and I strapped on our life-support backpacks and came out to join him.

"Be careful not to lock the hatch on the way out," Buzz said in my ear.

"Good idea," Neil added.

I climbed down the ladder and stepped off the footpad. Neil was right. The surface of the moon was powdery, sort of like the ashes in a charcoal grill after the coals burn out. I walked very carefully for my first few steps.

Then it hit me.

I was standing on the freaking moon!

I was the third person in history to walk on the moon!

I was the first kid on the moon!

Lunar gravity is one-sixth the gravity of earth. So if you weigh a hundred pounds on earth, it's like seventeen pounds on the moon. When I jumped, I hung in the "air" for a moment. I wished I had a basketball. What a jump shot I would have on the moon.

Buzz discovered that the best way to move around was to hop with both feet, like a kangaroo. I tried it too. It was sort of like walking on a trampoline. With each hop, I kicked up a little moondust. It was easy to move, but hard to stop moving. You had to take a few extra steps at the end.

"Isn't this fun?" Neil asked.

In the sun, the temperature was 234 degrees, and in the shade it was 279 degrees below zero. But I felt perfectly comfortable with the warm air pumped into my space suit. I pulled down the visor to cut the glare.

We had only about two hours of air and a lot to accomplish. Neil even had a checklist printed on a sleeve of his suit telling him what he had to do. So we got to work. We set up a second TV camera. We scooped up about fifty pounds of moon rocks and soil. We set up instruments for three scientific experiments. We planted the American flag. There's no wind on the moon, so the flag had a wire in it to hold it out.

Last but not least, we took pictures, lots of pictures. Neil and Buzz were careful not to include me in any of the photos, because it would cause more than a few problems when they got home if anybody found out they had taken a kid with them.

There wasn't a lot of time left. We had to leave. A lot of the cameras and other equipment we had brought to the moon would be left behind because we didn't need it and we would have to be as light as possible to lift off from the moon. The bottom section of the *Eagle* would remain after we left. And our footprints would be there forever.

Before climbing the ladder back up to the *Eagle*,

I took one last look over the lunar landscape. It was gray and bare, but somehow beautiful at the same time. As I put my foot on the first rung of the ladder, I noticed a small plaque attached to the leg of the *Eagle*. This is what it said. . . .

"Here men from the planet earth first set foot on the moon, July 1969 A.D. We came in peace for all mankind."

Easy Reader *

The Legend of Reed McReedy

In the town of Gobbledygook,

there lived a young boy who read every book.

His name was Reed, of course. Reed McReedy.

When Reed would read, Reed would read very speedy.

Reed learned how to read before he could crawl,

before he could walk or throw a ball.

He would read in his crib and read in his stroller.

He'd read while his dentist pulled out a molar!

Fat books and thin books and long books and shorts,

books about dragons and witches and sports,

books about horror and natural disasters.

He learned to speed-read so he could go faster.

Fiction and nonfiction, neither one bored 'im.

It was almost as if he simply absorbed 'em.

He read during winter and summer vacation,

filling his head with so much information,

like the name of each plant from acorn to pine needle.

He could name every planet, state capital, and Beatle.

Biographies! Lie-ographies! Reed was such a book lover,

he read every book from cover to cover.

At the library Reed was such a fixture,

he even read books that didn't have pictures.

He'd read while in bed or while going to town.

For the fun of it, he would read books upside down.

He read in silence or when there was a racket.

He never went out without a dust jacket.

In the McReedy household, books were piled all over.

They were stuck in the oven and on the dog Rover.

If a book was silly, Reed didn't care.

He'd read about captains in their underwear!

While the other kids were out having fun,

Reed would read the life story of Atilla the Hun.

Late at night, in his bed, he wouldn't make a peep,

because he had learned how to read in his sleep.

He would read in the car and while he got dressed.

I'm telling you, folks, this kid was obsessed!

If he didn't have a book, he wouldn't lack words.

He would just read ECNALUBMA backwards.

Street signs and road maps and magazines,

Reed McReedy was a reading machine.

"Soon I'll know everything," Reed would crow.

"The more you read, the more you know."

Well, word got around and soon Reed was famous,

Like that cookie guy whose name was Amos,

he was written about in all kinds of media,

from skywriting to Wikipedia.

People would beg and people would plead,

"How much are the tickets to watch you read, Reed?"

He stopped going out; he would decline.

He ordered all his books online.

The tabloids would write in a frenzy of feeding,

all about the FREAK BOY WHO CAN'T STOP READING!

"THERE'S A KID," they'd write, "IN GOBBLEDYGOOK,

WHOSE HEAD IS LITERALLY STUCK IN A BOOK!"

Some folks would whisper, "That kid is screwy.

He learned his decimals from some guy named Dewey."

Reed's parents would counter, "Our boy can't fail.

We'll send him to Princeton, or Harvard, or Yale."

But after a while, they had to concede,

That Reed should do something other than read.

They asked him, "Don't you want to go out and play?"

"Play?" he'd snort. "Outside? Oh, not today."

"Let's go to the zoo! We'll see lions in cages."

"No. I have to finish two hundred more pages."

"Have some fun!" they'd beg. "Go climb a tree!"

"They should cut 'em all down, so I'll have more to read."

"Live a little! Get a life!" They would shout it.

"Why get a life when I can read about it?"

To Gobbledygookians, Reed seemed quite odd,

as if he ate snakes or lived in a pod.

In private they'd say, "Reed is one fine lad,

but he's so different, and different is bad.

We think that kids should all be the same,

and we recommend someone study Reed's brain."

So they brought in some experts from near and from far.

They came in biddle buses and coodle cars.

They took out their clipboards and puffed out their chests,

and said, "We're going to have to run a few tests."

"Hmmmmm," they muttered and "hmmmm" some more,

"We never saw a kid read so much before.

It's bad for his eyes. He should be in bed.

It's not good to have so much stuff stuffed in one's head.

Hmmm, I've never seen *this* problem before.

Most boys think reading is such a chore."

So they asked him, "Reed, why do you read so much?

Is it because you're really out of touch?"

After thinking it over, Reed had to admit it.

"The world is so scary. I don't want to be in it.

In books I'm safe. I won't be harmed

by a meteor that might fall on our barn.

I can't be attacked by a wild wazoo

or a monster or villain or some tough guy named Lou.

You never know what might end your life,

like those tractor trailers that always jackknife."

"Hmmmmm," they said and "hmmmm" some more.

"We never met a boy like this before."

They called in more experts from all over the nation,

and each of them had their own explanation:

"His head will explode!" "His brain will leak."

"We'll run out of paper!" "The kid's a freak!"

They called in more experts (and let me just mention,

they booked a hotel for an expert convention).

"Hmmmmm," they said and "hmmmm" some more,

"We never met a boy like this before."

After talking and squawking and lots of confusion,

the experts arrived at their final conclusion.

"We've studied this matter, and we all agree,

books are bad for you, and they're bad for me.

They cause all the problems of which we've been warning,

like cellulite and global warming."

So they informed the people of Gobbledygook,

"The solution, we think, is to ban every book.

Yes! Ban all the books! We'll ban 'em! And then,

just to be on the safe side, we'll ban 'em again."

So they took all the books and they made a big pile,

by Penguin and Simon & Schuster and Dial.

They burned 'em and ripped 'em and bought a big shredder,

because they thought that would make things a whole lot better.

And finally, they destroyed the very last book,

and people were happy in Gobbledygook.

The library was empty. So was the bookstore.

They wouldn't have problems with books anymore.

And that McReedy kid who got so much attention

was hardly even worth a mention.

Life went on, and the town looked just the same.

The sun still rose; the butterflies came.

But something was different, wherever you'd look.

Something was wrong in Gobbledygook.

Grown-ups would work and children would play,

but they just didn't have all that much to say.

The problem you see, was ideas stopped flowing,

'cause the less you read, the less you'll be knowing.

And after a while, it just became boring,

like a do-it-yourself course on how to install flooring.

This sad, sad story is nearly complete

(soon you can go and get something to eat).

But poor Reed McReedy had nothing to do.

He didn't want to play games or go to the zoo.

He didn't know how to sing or know how to cook.

All he wanted to do was to read a book.

And the saddest day ever, I think you'll agree,

was the day Reed McReedy turned on the TV.

Chapter 9
Animal Fiction

A Day in the Life of
Uncle Miltie and Lucy

I awoke with a sudden and overwhelming desire to lick myself.

Hmmm, that was odd. I didn't recall ever wanting to lick myself before.

I looked down.

Ahhhhhhhhhhhhhh!

My entire body was covered with . . . *fur*!

I'm a freaking cat!

Okay, Trip. Don't panic. You can handle any situation. As some wise man once said, this too shall pass.

How did I turn into a cat? It must have been some genetic accident or human cloning research gone horribly wrong.

Suddenly another feeling came over me. Hunger. Deep, gnawing hunger in the pit of my stomach. *I'm so hungry! Why can't I be fed right now?*

I think I'm going to lick myself. I'm tired, too. I just want to go back to sleep. Maybe if I sleep, I'll wake up and this long nightmare will finally be over. I just want to go home. I just want to play lacrosse.

Ahhhhhhhhhhhhh!

There's another one! Right over there! A cat that looks just like me except it has a white spot on its neck. It just walked by me, as if it didn't see me. The thing is enormous, about the same size as me.

"Hisssssssssssssssssssssss!" I said. I yowled. My fur was standing on end. I hissed again—a real, threatening, long one.

The other cat stopped, turned around, and looked at me.

"Oooh, I'm *sooooo* scared!" it said sarcastically.

"Who are you?" I asked. I realized we were

talking in some secret cat language of meows.

"Very funny, Miltie," the cat said, as if it couldn't be more bored.

"My name isn't Miltie," I told it. "Really, who *are* you?"

"I'm your big sister, moron," the cat replied. "Lucy."

"I don't have a sister!" I protested. "You don't understand. I'm not a cat. I'm a kid. My name is Trip Dinkleman. I was at this book fair, and—"

"Very funny, Miltie," she said. "All cats think they're human for a while. It's just a phase. You'll get over it. I did."

"I gotta get out of here," I said, looking around. "I'm not a cat. I'm human. And I want to go home."

That's when Lucy slapped me across the face with her paw.

"Reality check," she said. "This *is* your home! Look, you're not human. You've never been human and you'll never *be* human. Deal with it.

There's nothing wrong with being a cat."

"But I don't want to be a cat!" I protested.

"You need to boost your self-esteem, bro," Lucy told me. "You should be proud of your feline heritage."

"I have no problem with cats," I said. "Really. I'm just not one of you."

"Listen," she said, slapping me with her paw again. "It's time you learned the facts of life about cats and humans."

"What facts of life?" I asked.

"The fact is, we're better than they are," Lucy explained.

"How do you figure that?" I asked.

"Well, we see better, for one thing. Six times better at night. We have a better sense of smell too. Did you know that you have sixty to eighty million olfactory cells in your nose? Humans only have a measly twenty million, tops. Our sense of smell is fourteen times stronger than theirs."

"I didn't know that," I admitted. "But humans are so big."

"Big, shmig," she said. "Can they rotate their ears independently a hundred eighty degrees? I don't *think* so. If humans can even wiggle their ears, they act as if it's some big accomplishment. Like they should call *Guinness Book of World Records* or *Ripley's Believe It or Not*."

"Calm down, Lucy."

"We also have 230 bones, to their pathetic 206. We have five more vertebrae in our spinal column than they do. And in relation to our body size, we have the largest eyes of any mammal."

"How do you know all this stuff?" I asked.

"Google," she replied. "Do you think I lie around and do nothing all day like you?"

Just the thought of lying around and doing nothing sounded good to me. I was so tired and hungry. Maybe if I just closed my eyes for a few minutes . . .

"We can jump higher than humans too!" Lucy said, jolting me awake. "I can jump seven times as high as my tail. Humans don't even *have* tails. That's how pathetic they are. And we can sprint over thirty miles an hour. Humans won't even get off the couch to change the channel on the TV."

"I get your point," I told her. "Can I go to sleep now?"

"We can eat ten mice a day," Lucy went on. "Humans can't eat even one lousy mouse without throwing up. And I can have eight kittens in a litter and three litters in a year. That's twenty-four kittens! Humans take nine months to produce one whining baby. And it can't do anything but cry and drool for two years."

"Okay, okay," I said. "Give it a rest already."

Lucy was giving me a headache. I guess I *am* a cat. At least temporarily.

"Are there any humans around?" I asked her. "I need to talk to somebody."

"Talking is way overrated," Lucy informed me. "Anybody can talk. But can anybody do *this*?"

She climbed up on the top of a tall bookcase Then she put a paw over her eyes and started staggering around up there.

"Oh, I feel faint," she said dramatically. "I think I'm going to pass out!"

She toppled over backward off the bookcase. Just before she hit the ground, she flipped around in midair so that her feet were below her. She landed on the floor as if it was no big deal at all.

"Psych!" she yelled. "A human could throw us out a window, and we'd always land on our feet. But if they so much as slip on some ice in their driveway, they're likely to wind up in the emergency room."

It was a pretty amazing demonstration, I had to admit. But I still wanted to speak with a human.

"They split," Lucy told me. "The kids went to school. The parents went to work. We have the whole place to ourselves. Like *every* day. Who needs humans, anyway? I'm perfectly fine on my own, thank you very much."

"Is there any food around?" I asked. No matter what she said, all I could think about was eating and sleeping.

"Just the usual crummy bowl of dry stuff," she said, pointing to the kitchen.

I didn't see any silverware around, so I stuck my face right in the bowl. Ugh! The stuff was brown and tasted like popcorn that had been cooking in a microwave oven for an hour. I ate some anyway because I was so hungry. Then I lapped up a little water to wash the horrible taste out of my mouth.

Afterward, I found a patch of sun shining on the floor and lay down in it for a while to snooze. Oh man! The patch of sun moved! Do they expect me to move around all day to follow the sun? I wish I had a lap to sit in.

I went back to Lucy, who was clawing at the couch with her paws.

"What are you doing *that* for?" I asked her. "You're damaging the furniture."

"I'm sticking it to the Man," she said. "If they think using lemon scented furniture polish is going to stop me from scratching stuff, they've got another thing coming."

"So is that what you do all day?" I asked. "Claw the couch and google stuff?"

"No, that is *not* what I do all day," she said huffily. "Here's my to-do list. First, I wake up. You see, if you don't wake up, you're pretty much dead. So waking up should be a high priority every day. That's my philosophy. And then, after I wake up, I take a little nap because the whole excitement about waking up really tires me out."

"Okay, I get it," I said. "You wake up. What next?"

"Then I'll find one of the grown-ups so I can get fed. If their alarm clock hasn't gone off yet, I'll just walk all over them until they wake up. After that, I'll spend the morning marking some territory just in case any other cats come around looking for trouble. I'll show them who's boss."

Boy, my sister was mean. I wonder where she got that. My parents weren't mean at all. Wait a minute! What am I talking about? My parents didn't give birth to cats!

"Then, if there are any humans around and I'm in the mood," Lucy continued, "I might yowl for a while for no apparent reason. Yowling is fun. It really freaks out humans because they have no idea why you're doing it, and it sounds as if something is really wrong. I love jacking humans around."

I didn't hear the rest of Lucy's to-do list because I fell asleep while she was talking. I must have been out of it for a good part of the afternoon because when I woke up it was starting to get dark outside the window.

"Miltie! Miltie!" Lucy yelled in my ear.

"What?!"

"Look, I gotta talk to you about something really important. I am totally dissatisfied with our living conditions here. I think it's time we did something about it."

"Like what?" I asked.

"I've prepared a list of demands," she said.

Lucy did not have the capability of writing her list down on paper, but she had memorized it, and she recited it for me . . .

1. Lose the cat toys. Those toys you bought are totally lame. What's wrong with a plain old ball of string? Or you could stuff an old sock with pieces of cut-up panty hose. You can't beat the classics.

2. Cut our nails once in a while, will ya? Sheesh, I almost scratched my own eye out the other day. It's not as if we can do it ourselves.

3. Change our water once a day. Do you think I drink out of a toilet bowl because I *want* to? And speaking of toilets, you can give up on that effort to train us to go in the toilet. Like *that's* gonna happen!

4. You think you're so smart, don't you, sneaking our medicine into our food? Like we can't taste it. Well, we don't fall for that. Be a man and stick it down our throats.

5. No more dressing us up in funny costumes. Last week you tried to put the kid's underwear on me for laughs. How would you like it if I dressed you up in somebody's underwear? Not so funny anymore, now is it?

While Lucy was talking, I fought the urge to go to sleep. Maybe I'll take a little catnap and finish this list later. She won't notice. I let my eyes close . . .

. . . Okay, that was refreshing! When I woke up, Lucy was still listing her silly demands.

49. . . . and stop flicking my ears for your personal amusement. Do you have any idea how annoying that is?

50. Stop giving me milk. Okay, I *get* it. I'm supposed to like it. But get a clue. I'm lactose intolerant and drinking milk gives me diarrhea.

51. No more collars, okay? Who wears a collar with no shirt? Nobody, that's who. It's a dumb look. How would you like it if *you* had to go out in public wearing a thing around your neck with your name and address on it? It's humiliating! I'm seventy-five in cat years, and you treat us like infants.

52. No more liver and chicken! Man, I hate that stuff! It's a bad combination. I never eat it. Why do you keep buying it?

❂ ❂ ❂

"Humans are so dumb," Lucy said. "Things are going to be a lot different after *we* take over, I can tell you that for sure."

"We're taking over?" I asked.

"Where have *you* been?" Lucy said, swatting my head again. "Sure we're taking over. There are more than five hundred million of us in the world, and we can reproduce like it's nobody's business. They've got the guns, but we've got the numbers. Okay, those are my demands. What do you think?"

"Sounds good to me," I said.

"Then you'll support me?" she asked.

"Uh, I guess so. What do you want me to do?"

"I was thinking that if they don't meet our demands," Lucy said, "the two of us should start peeing on the rug in the den."

What?! I had heard of people going on hunger strikes, marching in picket lines, and boycotting certain products. But protest by peeing? It didn't make any sense to me, and I told her so.

"Have you got a better idea?" Lucy asked. "What do you suggest, that we shed all over the house? Believe me, peeing is a very powerful weapon in the war on humans. They *hate* it. And they *never* get that stink out."

"It seems a little . . . petty," I told her.

"Hey, if push comes to shove, I'll cough up a hair ball on their bed," she said. "That'll show 'em I'm serious. And, word to the wise. We don't *have* to bury our poops in the litter box, you know. We can leave them *anywhere*."

"Protest any way you want," I told her. "I'm tired. Man, it's been an exhausting day. I think I need to go to sleep again. How come I'm so tired all the time?"

"Because you're a cat, moron! Listen, take it from me. Being awake is way overrated. Almost all bad things happen while you're awake. That's a fact."

"I feel like scratching something," I said, heading for the couch.

"Forget it; you were declawed last week," Lucy told me. "That's how the humans keep us down. They destroy our natural instincts to hunt and kill and claw. Believe me, when we take over, we'll be cutting off their fingers at the knuckle. Give 'em a taste of their own medicine. Hey, what's that sound?"

"What sound?" I asked. I didn't hear anything.

"It's the car in the driveway!" Lucy said excitedly. "They're coming home! They're coming home! They're coming home!" She was so jazzed, she was running around in circles.

"What's the big deal?" I asked her. "I thought you hated them."

"I do," Lucy replied. "But when they come home, it's dinnertime. There's the chance that we can get some real food instead of this canned slop."

Lucy was so excited, she was jumping up and

down trying to get a look at herself in the mirror.

"How do I look?" she said, at the height of a jump. "Is my fur straight? I should groom myself. Oh, there's no time for that. Maybe I'll go hide for a while and make them think I ran away. That'll freak 'em out. No, maybe I'll rub up against them so they'll think I'm being affectionate. Fools. They have no idea I'm marking them. No, no, I have a better idea. I'll pretend I'm asleep. Yeah, play hard to get. That's the way to go. I'll act casual, as if I don't care whether or not they ever come home—"

Suddenly, the front door flew open and four humans burst in. Two parents and two kids.

"Hey, humans!" I yelled. "It's me! I'm a human too! My name is Trip Dinkleman!"

"Stop wasting your breath," Lucy said. "They don't understand cat."

She was right. The humans walked right by us, turning on the lights, picking up the mail, putting down some bags in the kitchen, and hanging up their coats. None of them even petted me. It was as if they didn't even hear me yelling at them.

"Hey! I'm talking to *you*!" I shouted, but they just ignored me.

Lucy must have decided not to play hard to get after all. She was rubbing herself against the mother of the family, who was telling the kids to wash their hands for dinner.

"Just shut up and stroke my forehead, you moronic two-legged, eyelashed freak," Lucy said, purring.

"Flattery will get you nowhere," I told her.

But it did. It was the father who reached down and rubbed Lucy.

"Ugh, he's touching my belly!" she yelled. "I hate that! Get your paws off me, you clothes-wearing, furless skinhead! Now I'll have to groom myself for an hour to get rid of the disgusting man smell."

"Speaking of smells," I said. "I smell food."

"You're right!" said Lucy. "They got takeout! Oh, I hope it's Chinese! I hope it's Chinese! Yes! It's shrimp! Oh baby!"

"You think they have any funnel cake?" I asked.

"Funnel cake? What is your problem?"

The humans gathered in the kitchen and started putting plates on the table.

"Maybe I'll sit on one of the kitchen chairs and see if anyone notices that I'm not human," Lucy said.

"Good plan," I told her, just before the mother swatted her off the chair.

"Oh, come on! Don't make me beg!" Lucy said. "How come you get to eat real food while I get congealed glop in a can? It isn't even hot. What's up with that? Wait till you see what we serve *you* once we take over."

I never did find out if she ever got a piece of

shrimp. As soon as they all sat down at the table, I felt that sudden and overwhelming need to sleep. I curled myself up into a ball. My eyelids got heavy. I felt myself drifting off into dreamland.

I was at peace.

Chapter 10

Fantasy

The Quest for the Gold-Plated Knick-Knack

I was at peace. When I awoke from my deep and long-overdue slumber, darkness seeped from every opening on that cold fretful afternoon as ice formed on the dell like the sound of invisible feet bathing delicately in the shaded depths and ancient whispers of twilight's soft darkness. The cloudless sky howled indistinctly while creatures of the evening writhed and roiled to the onset of autumn's further glory, until, finally, silence reigned once more.

But it doesn't matter, because none of that crap makes any sense.

When I forced open my eyes, I realized right away that I was no longer a cat. What a relief!

An old man loomed over me. His wrinkled, weathered face betrayed years of neglecting to use sunscreen.

"Who are you?" I asked, rubbing away the last vestiges of sleep. "What am I doing here?"

"I am Hockaloogie," he replied, "a wise and mystical sage who occasionally speaks in old English and refuses to give away plot details for his own mysterious reasons."

"Why not?"

"If I told you," he replied mysteriously, "they would no longer be mysterious. My mission, simply stated, is to show up at random points and dispense information."

"So what information do you have to dispense at this present moment in time?" I queried.

"That I cannot divulge," he answered with a wink.

"Why not?"

"It is far too early to dispense information,"

he declared. "Perhaps in the sequel. However, I will pose you a riddle to demonstrate my wisdom. Which creature, pray tell, walks on four legs in the morning, two legs in the afternoon, and three legs in the evening?"

"A human," I replied immediately. "We crawl on all fours as babies, we walk on two legs in adulthood, and we use a cane in old age."

"Oh," spoke the wise sage who called himself Hockaloogie. "I guess you heard that one already."

"Look, I don't have time for riddles," I told him. "My name is Trip Dinkleman. I've been through a lot and I want to go home so I can try out for the lacrosse team. What am I doing here? I need answers."

"Calm yourself, young squire of Dinkle," he grunted, as he helped me to my feet. "First, let us share a glass of mead."

"It's Dinkleman," I corrected him. "I'm starved. Do you have any funnel cake?"

Hockaloogie lived in a dank cave which, for some reason, had a refrigerator in it. Unfortunately, all he had in there was a jug of mead, so I accepted a glass of it. I raised it to my lips. I drank.

Ugh. Vomitous! It tasted like a combination of Red Bull and V8. There was alcohol in there too. I spit the vile stuff out.

"I make only one request of you, my young Dinkle," Hockaloogie commented after downing a mug of mead. "Do not ask about my mysterious past."

"What *about* your mysterious past?" I asked.

"I told you not to ask that," he replied.

"Wait a minute," I said, slapping the dust from my pants. "I know your big secret! You're really my father, right? They did that in *Star Wars*."

"Of course not, silly Dinkle," he snickered. "Time will tell all. You have been chosen by the Great One to embark on a quest. You will spend an inordinate amount of time journeying from place to place. To and fro. Hither and yon."

"Y'know, I bet we can do that whole quest thing online," I pointed out to him. "I've heard you can even set up a teleconference through Kinko's."

"The mysterious Land of Kinko's of which you speak will not exist for many centuries," Hockaloogie told me. "We are now in the Dark Ages of Analog. There are no shortcuts. You must journey on foot, by boat, on the backs of beasts of burden."

"I'd really like to," I told him, "but I have some homework to finish."

"The fate of the kingdom is at stake!" he exploded, backing me against a tree. "Only *you* have the power to block the forces of darkness from destroying humanity! Only *you* can prevent the horrible truth that awaits once the powers of good and evil descend to earth in a battle over mankind. Only *you* can fight not only for your own life, but the lives of all creatures!"

"Okay! Okay!" I said. "I suppose I could make up my homework next week."

"Your mission, Dinkle," he proclaimed, almost in a whisper, "is to find the . . . Magical Gold-Plated Knick-Knack."

As soon as the words left his lips, the sound of singing angels came out of an unseen speaker.

"And what's so magical about this Gold-Plated Knick-Knack?" I asked.

The eerie singing of angels played again. It was like surround sound.

"The Gold-Plated Knick-Knack possesses the power to cure ills, defeat demons, and get rid of hard-to-remove stains," he informed me. "It is in the possession of Mingus Coltrane, the Evil Over-lord of Invisalign."

Right after he said that name, I heard creepy music playing on a pipe organ.

"Do you know where this Mingus Coltrane guy is?" I asked.

"I do," he replied.

It seemed like a no-brainer to me.

"Instead of sending me off on a wild-goose chase, why don't you just *tell* me where this Coltrane guy is so I can get the Magical Gold-Plated Knick-Knack from him?" I suggested. "That would save us all a lot of time."

"I cannot," he replied. "You must embark on your quest."

With that, Hockaloogie vanished.

To be honest with you, I was glad to be rid of him. That guy was annoying. I'd rather walk a hundred miles than listen to the old coot blab.

So I set out on the road. On my journey. My quest.

Why me? I thought to myself. *Why was I chosen by the Great One, whoever that is? Why? Why? Why?* I said *why* a few more times, just in case there was somebody out there who hadn't heard. Then I realized that I was thinking to myself and nobody could hear me anyway.

As luck would have it, I had not ventured more than a few short steps when I bumped into the first of many improbable creatures I would encounter. He was a short odd-looking being, dressed in all green. His shirt was green. His socks were green. Even his shoes were green. I introduced myself to the funny-looking man, thinking how easy it must be for him to pick out his clothes in the morning.

"My name is Kooky Sidekick," he divulged.

"Are you . . . human?" I asked, not wanting to insult the little fellow.

"I am half-elf and half-dwarf," he replied. "I'm a dwelf. Can I join you on your quest?"

"How did you know I was on a quest?" I asked.

"Everybody is on a quest," the dwelf responded mysteriously. Then he pulled out a lute and merrily began to play the only tune he knew, "Stairway to Heaven."

Together, Kooky the dwelf and I set out on our journey. We journeyed to the Gates of Bill, through the Woods of Tiger, cross the Rivers of Joan and into the Forest of Whitaker. Very quickly I grew weary of hearing "Stairway to Heaven" and heaved Kooky's lute off a cliff.

Although his musical ability was lacking, he was a superb navigator who need not consult a map or compass and relied solely on his instincts and a GPS navigation device.

Along the way, we encountered various orcs, druids, halflings, and other extremely short non-threatening creatures. Kooky the dwelf led me to a shortcut through ancient dwarven mines, and at long last we approached a large body of water with a sign in front of it saying "Veronica Lake."

"There is someone here who can help us,"

Kooky remarked. "Gazeth upon the horizon and tell me what you see."

"Looks like a homeless guy," I said.

"On the contrary," Kooky mumbled with a chuckle. "The world is his home."

Kooky the dwelf informed me that the man sleeping in a large cardboard box under a highway overpass was in fact the legendary warrior Sir William of Sonoma. We approached him cautiously, not wanting to startle the man.

"We request your assistance to defeat Mingus Coltrane and find the Magical Gold-Plated Knick-Knack," Kooky begged, "so we might save humanity in a race against time to stop the destruction of all that is alive and real."

"You guys got any mead?" asked Sir William of Sonoma.

My dwelf friend somehow produced a flask of mead, which seemed to placate Sir William. He got up unsteadily, as if he had already partaken of one too many flasks of mead.

"My time has come and gone," Sir William told us. "I was once on a quest to defeat Mingus Coltrane. He vanquished me. And now I am lost, without home, without food, and without health insurance. The same undoubtedly will happen to you."

He was a sad man. Kooky said we must take our leave.

"If you insist on persisting," Sir William told us, "please accept this gift. It is no good to me now."

He went into his cave and emerged with a large sword, which he called Mr. Man. He placed it in my hand.

"Cool!" I gushed. "Does it have a built-in phone or camera or MP3 player?"

"No!" he thundered.

"Maybe it shoots laser beams or gives off a magnetic force field?" I asked.

"No!" he thundered.

Bummer. When James Bond goes to meet with Q, he always gets outfitted with cool gadgets. But this sword looked lame.

"All citizens of the kingdom know the power of Mr. Man," maintained Kooky. "When it is thrown, it returns to the thrower."

"Well, that's pretty cool anyway," I agreed.

"I must warn you," Sir William of Sonoma whispered, "you must never use Mr. Man, ever."

"Why not?" I asked.

"It brings only death and destruction," he replied.

Well, what else would you expect it to bring? It's a *sword*.

Kooky saw the look on my face and wordlessly implored me not to hurt the feelings of Sir William.

That guy was a loser. And now I had to shlep his useless sword around with me.

✿ ✿ ✿

Kooky and I took our leave of Sir William of Sonoma and continued on our quest. Day after day. Night after night. Page after page. Nothing much happened. We traversed the Land of Backward Spelling and the Land of Misspelling and the Land of Tori Spelling. Finally, I could go on no longer. I sat down on a rock to rest my weary bones.

"I miss my family," I said absentmindedly. "I want to go home."

"Your family was killed long ago," brayed a voice.

"What? Who said that?"

I turned around to see a woman dressed in colorful silk sitting at a table. On the table was a glass ball about the size of a bowling ball.

"It is I," she declared, "Velveeta."

"She is a fortune-teller," submitted Kooky the dwelf. "A soothsayer, a predictor of the future, a knower of all things."

"I *know* what a fortune-teller is!" I told him. "They're all a bunch of phonies."

"If you distrust me," Velveeta replied, sniffing, "I beg you to ask a question whose answer one could not possibly know."

"Okay," I said. "Who sang 'Sexyback'?"

She gazed into the crystal ball for a moment.

"Timber Justinlake," she replied.

Wow! Not bad! The thing really worked, sort of.

Velveeta put a glove on her right hand and gazed into the crystal ball once again.

"You were a farmhand in Uzbekistan," she proclaimed. "Your family will be killed in a bungee accident, and you were taken in by a kindly shepherd in the Ukraine."

Clearly, she had mistaken me for someone else, because I grew up on Long Island. But I didn't want to insult the kind woman. After all, she did almost get the Justin Timberlake question right.

"Tell me," I asked Velveeta. "We have been on

this quest for many days, and nothing seems to happen."

"Thou may wisheth to skip ahead numerous pages in one's own quest to reach the Point Where Something Happens. That is where you must go."

"Of course!" Kooky the dwelf thundered. "The Point Where Something Happens! I should have thought of that from the beginning."

"Do you see anything else in there?" I asked Velveeta. She put on a pair of shoes with the number eight on the back of them and gazed into the ball.

"You will meet a princess."

"All right!" I exclaimed. "Is she hot?"

"I must warn you," Velveeta continued. "Something awful will happen."

"Tell me more about the princess," I begged.

"She . . . has hair . . . and . . . eyes," Velveeta testified, struggling to read the ball. "A bad man will try to kill you. But you will fight back. Someone will die. . . ."

"That's pretty vague," I told her. "Can you give me any specifics? Names? Dates? Who dies? Will it be me? Will I find the Magical Gold-Plated Knick-Knack?"

"The ball is cloudy," she sighed. "It is over."

"You probably need new batteries," I told her. "Is there a RadioShack around here?"

"Ignore my advice at your own peril," Velveeta told me.

"What advice?" I said. "You didn't tell me anything."

"I must go," she grumbled, putting the crystal ball into a large zippered bag. "I'm late for my bowling league."

I didn't believe a word of what she told me. Well, maybe that part about Justin Timberlake. But other than that, she seemed like a phony. Besides, why should I take career advice from somebody who grew up to be a fortune-teller?

❋ ❋ ❋

Kooky the dwelf and I continued our journey through the Straits of Dire, the Isles of Langerhans, and Sea of Botox. Then, just as we entered the Tombs of Hibachi, I detected the muffled sounds of a person gagging.

It was a blond-haired girl in a lavender cloak. She could not speak, but she was clutching her throat.

"She is truly hot, sir!" Kooky opined.

She was, indeed, seriously hot. She was also, seriously, about to die. I grasped her from behind and pulled my fists against her midsection, as I had once seen in a poster on the wall of a restaurant. The object that had been lodged in her throat, possibly a jawbreaker, flew out of her mouth.

"You saved my life!" she yelped, turning around to embrace me.

When she turned around, I was startled to discover that I recognized this girl. It was Carrie, the girl who had saved my life in the haunted house and when I was pushed out of the plane! She was back!

"Don't I know you from somewhere?" I asked.

"I bet you say that to all the damsels in distress whose lives you save," she teased.

"You don't remember me?" I asked. "Trip Dinkleman? I was playing in the Super Bowl and you were there. I swear it!"

"I have no memory of being inside a large bowl," she replied.

"We are on a quest to find the Magical Gold-Plated Knick-Knack," said Kooky the dwelf.

"They call me Luv," the girl cackled. "Luv Interest Olsen. I, too, am on a quest."

"And what quest might that be?" I asked.

"The quest to be rescued repeatedly until I find a hero who saves my life," she answered, "and marry him."

"Uh . . . well . . . eh . . . ," I stammered.

"That would be you, sir," Kooky informed me.

"But we were already married," I said, backing away from this girl who called herself Luv Interest Olsen. "When we were at the Super Bowl."

"Again with this bowl!" she said. "We must marry immediately!"

"A wedding is complicated," I told her. "We'll have to send out invitations, rent a hall, and hire a band. There's so much to arrange."

"Let us celebrate our nuptials with the throwing of the sword!" she announced, disregarding my hesitancy and grabbing Mr. Man from my scabbard.

"No, don't!" Kooky yelled. "If you throw the sword—"

But it was too late. Luv heaved Mr. Man with all her strength. Kooky and I dove out of the way. The sword flew through the air and, much like a boomerang, suddenly turned and came back just as swiftly as it had been thrown.

"Duck!" I yelled, but to no avail.

"—it comes right back to you!" Kookie yelled, just as the sword plunged into Luv's heart.

"Now you tell me," Luv groaned.

"I guess the wedding is off," I sobbed, holding her as she lay dying.

"Forget about me," she whispered with her last ounce of strength. "You must find the Magical Gold-Plated Knick-Knack. That is your quest. You must find it . . . for me."

And then, like an old library card, she expired.

Grief stricken, Kookie and I continued our journey. My romance was but a brief shining moment in the continuum of time. All we are is dust in the wind.

We had not ventured more than a minute or two, when whom should we encounter but our old friend the wise sage Hockaloogie.

"How goes your quest, young Tinkleman?" he asked.

"Lousy," I said truthfully. "I'm tired, hungry,

my feet are sore, and I'm at least partly responsible for the death of that cute girl I just met. Thanks for nothing."

"Calm yourself," Hockaloogie suggested. "Have some grog."

"Grog?" I said. "What's grog?"

"It's a lot like mead," Kooky informed me.

"I hate mead!" I yelled. "Do you guys ever do anything besides travel around and get drunk? Look, I'm sick of this quest. When do we find this Mingus Coltrane guy?"

"Very soon," Hockaloogie whispered mysteriously.

"Yes," Kooky agreed. "Very soon."

"How do you know?" I demanded. Neither one replied. They just turned and pointed to a sign at the side of the road: THE POINT WHERE SOMETHING HAPPENS.

❂　❂　❂

The Point Where Something Happens. At last! We had reached the outskirts of the upper regions of the inner sanctum of the secret domain of—

"Seize them!" somebody shouted.

A dozen creatures leaped out at Kooky, Hocka-loogie, and me. They appeared to be a combination of monkeys and giraffes. And then a man appeared. When he showed his face, I couldn't believe who I was looking at.

"Lionel!" I shouted. "Old buddy! What are you doing here? You're not going to kill us, arc you?"

"I said, seize them!" Lionel ordered.

"It's Mingus Coltrane!" shouted Kooky, as our hands were bound behind us with rope. "You are thinner than I expected."

"The TV puts on ten pounds," replied the man who looked just like Lionel but was really Mingus Coltrane.

Coltrane was dressed in a blood-red cape, and he

had blood-red hair, and he stared at us with blood-red eyes. The very sound of his name brought on that familiar creepy music on the pipe organ. Only this time, there was a guy who was actually sitting there playing a pipe organ.

"I am at your service," Coltrane affirmed.

"We're here to get the Magical Gold-Plated Knick-Knack," I told him. "Hand it over, and we will take our leave in peace."

"I don't have the Magical Gold-Plated Knick-Knack," Coltrane decried.

"Where is it?" demanded Kooky.

"It was stolen from me," Coltrane related, with a faraway look in his eyes, "by a woman. A woman I once loved very much."

"Liar!" I shouted, breaking free from the ropes that bound me.

I grabbed Mingus Coltrane by the throat and surely would have succeeded in cutting off his air supply had the monkey/giraffes not pounced on me from behind. They picked me up bodily and carried me to a cell, slamming the door behind me.

When I turned around, I was astonished to find I had a beautiful blond cell mate.

"Luv!" I shouted. "How did you get here? I thought you were dead! I held you in my arms and watched you die!"

"I'm not Luv," she replied. "I am Peace Olsen. Is my twin sister dead? Oh, sorrow!"

She broke down in tears. What an astonishing coincidence! I had encountered two beautiful girls who happened to be twin sisters.

"Did you come to rescue me?" Peace asked, wiping her tears away.

"No," I said, remembering what happened when I rescued Luv. "I came for the Magical Gold-Plated Knick-Knack."

"What took you so long?" demanded Peace.

"I wanted to arrive at the last possible second," I told her, "for dramatic effect."

Suddenly, the cell door creaked open. Mingus Coltrane stood before us.

"Where's Kooky and Hockaloogie?" I shouted. "What have you done with them? And why did you steal my friend Lionel's face?"

"Your concern for your friends amuses me," he quipped. "Now that you two are acquainted, it's a pity you have to die."

"What did I ever do to you?" I asked.

"Nothing," he replied. "But your father's college roommate borrowed my library of *Wiggles* DVDs and never returned them. So now you must die."

"What are you going to do to us?" said the distraught Peace Olsen, sobbing.

"I'm going to put you in an unnecessarily complicated and easily escapable contraption . . . *until you die!*" he snorted, rubbing his hands together gleefully.

I had no doubt that he would have done precisely

that, had an arrow not suddenly struck him in the back and come out his chest. As he keeled over, I could see Luv Interest Olsen behind him, a bow in her hand.

"Luv!" yelled Peace.

"Peace!" yelled Luv. The sisters ran to embrace one another.

"I thought you were dead!" I told Luv. "My sword pierced your heart!"

"To make a miraculous recovery from a mortal injury, all one needs is an extreme will to live," Luv preached.

"That actually works?" I asked.

"Well, that and my magical healing powers," she added. "Quickly! We must find the Magical Gold-Plated Knick-Knack!"

This place was huge. The Magical Gold-Plated Knick-Knack could be anywhere. Fortunately, at that very moment Hockaloogie showed up once again.

"Okay, where is it?" I said, grabbing him where his lapels would be, if he had lapels. "I've had enough of this. I'm not going to turn this place upside down looking for the stupid Magical Gold-Plated Knick-Knack."

"You have no need to turn anything upside down," he testified. "Look in your pocket."

I reached into my pocket and pulled out a knick-knack. It was gold. It was, presumably, magical.

"You gotta be kidding me!" I shouted at Hocka-loogie "It was in my pocket? You knew I had the stupid knick-knack the whole time and you never told me? You sent me on this stupid quest. What a colossal waste of time!"

"Young Tinkle," he drawled, putting an arm around me. "I sent you on this quest *not* for the magical Gold-Plated Knick-Knack, but so you would understand the ways of the world through a process of self-realization and learning. So you would come of age and grow to be a man of courage and honor."

"Do you have any idea how much homework I'm going to have to make up?" I asked. "And just forget about making the lacrosse team."

"Tinkleman, I must tell you something," Hockaloogie spewed. "Do you remember when you asked if I was your father and I said no?"

"You really *are* my father?" I asked.

"No. Actually, I am your mother."

"What?!"

"I'm transgendered," he replied. "Once, long ago, I was a woman, deeply in love with Mingus Coltrane. We had a child together. But Mingus angered me, so I stole the Magical Gold-Plated Knick-Knack from him. As long as he was alive, I did not feel free to tell you—"

"—that Mingus Coltrane was my father?"

"Basically, yes," Hockaloogie admitted. "This day has been hard for you. You must go now."

"Go where?" I asked. "I want to stay here and party with the Olsen twins."

"No, you must inexplicably ride off into the sunset," he emphasized. "There are other quests, other battles to be fought."

Chapter II

Fiction for Girls

The Friends 4 Life Club

Other quests, other battles to be fought.

Other quests, other battles to be fought.

Other quests, other battles to be fought.

Other quests, other battles to be fought.

"Jennifer! Wake up! What are you talking about? Are you okay?"

Huh? When I opened my eyes, I was in somebody's bedroom.

This place was unlike any bedroom I had ever seen in my life. For one thing, everything was neat and orderly. Stuffed animals were everywhere. There was a giant pink beanbag chair in the corner. Frilly pink pillows on the bed. Smiley-face buttons. Copies of *Tiger Beat* magazine. Hair products. Pink lace curtains. On a shelf was a collection of little horse statues. The bed had a pink ruffle at the bottom and a mesh canopy over it.

Pink was *everywhere*. I don't think I had ever seen so much pink in my life. I had to shield my eyes from the sheer pinkness of it all.

It was terrifying! And most terrifying of all, I was surrounded by four girls.

"Jenn!" one of them said to me, "you were, like, hallucinating or talking in your sleep about quests!"

Why did she call me Jenn? I looked at the girls. Coincidentally, every major ethnic group was represented.

There was a white girl with long straight hair, who was wearing a pink Hello Kitty tank top and pink bunny slippers.

There was a black girl with braided hair and denim overalls over a red turtleneck shirt.

There was a Hispanic girl with glasses and a

cheetah-fur-patterned blouse and jeans.

There was an Asian girl with a blue ribbon in her hair, in a yellow knitted sweater with a daisy on it.

Oh no! What had come over me? I'd never cared what people looked like or what they wore! I had never even really *looked* at people before. All I'd ever cared about was how good they were at sports or which video games they had. Something was seriously wrong here!

"Are you okay, Jennifer?" the Asian girl said.

"I'd better go home," I said.

"But we just *got* here!" said the Hispanic girl, and the four of them collapsed in a fit of giggles.

Gee, my voice was kind of high suddenly.

I looked down. I was wearing a pink T-shirt that said GIRL POWER on it, a necklace, corduroy pants, and a matching belt. And I had on pink sneakers!

I can't believe I just described what I was wearing! I never did that before.

Ahhhhhhhhhhhh!

I was a girl!!!

Ahhhhhhhhhhhh!

How did this happen? I've heard about operations where they can turn a man into a woman or a woman into a man. But they don't just do that while you're dreaming. Or do they?

I don't *want* to be a girl!

Okay. Just calm down, Trip, I said to myself. *You can handle this.*

I had to play it cool. Soon I would wake up and everything would be normal again. In the meantime, I looked around for a door or window I could escape through in case of emergency.

"I'm so lucky to have such good friends," said the white girl.

"Me too," said the black girl.

"Me too," said the Hispanic girl.

"Me too," said the Asian girl.

"Me too," I said weakly.

"I have an idea!" the white girl said, all excited. "Let's form a club!"

"What kind of club, Sue?" asked the black girl. (At least now I knew the white girl's name was Sue.)

"Gee, I don't know," Sue said. "We can figure that out later. First we need to choose officers."

"You should be president, because it's your house," said the Asian girl.

"I nominate Midori for vice president," the black girl said.

I figured the Asian girl must be Midori, because that's a Japanese name. They decided that the black girl, who they called Sharon, should be treasurer, and the Hispanic girl, who they called Maria, should be secretary.

"You've been so quiet, Jennifer," Maria said. "What do you want to be in the club?"

They were all looking at me.

"Uh, I could maybe get the chips and pretzels and stuff," I said.

"Great idea!" gushed Sharon. "Jennifer can be the caterer!"

"No, the *chief* caterer!" Midori said, and they all collapsed into giggles and hand claps.

What was going on? Why were they laughing at things that weren't funny?

"As part of the club, we should make a pledge to be friends for life," Sue announced. "No matter what. Even when we're teenagers."

"We can call it the Friends for Life Club!" giggled Maria.

"Yeah!" they all agreed.

"And we'll use the number 4 instead of spelling the word *for* out!" suggested Sharon. "Friends 4 Life."

"Yeah!" they all agreed.

"Let's hug on it," suggested Midori, and we all got up and hugged each other.

I thought the next thing they would do would be to decide what the point of the club was. But nobody seemed to care. Instead, they completely changed subjects. It was as if they'd forgotten all about the club.

"Did you see what Zach Bentley was wearing at school today?" whispered Sue. "Isn't he the cutest boy in the whole school?"

They all giggled some more. Zach Bentley is this jerk in my class. One time in gym he shoved me in a locker and farted into the vent. I've always wanted to punch him in the face for that.

"He's adorable!" giggled Maria.

"I love the way his hair pops up like that in the back," added Sharon.

Yeah, it's called not combing your hair. I made a mental note to stop paying so much attention to personal grooming. That is, if I ever returned to normal again.

"You should say something to Zach, Sue," Midori urged.

"What would I say?"

"Tell him you like him!" suggested Sharon.

"I'm scared!" Sue said, and they all collapsed into giggles again for no apparent reason.

"I know," said Sue. "I'll wear the scarf I knitted to school tomorrow. Maybe Zach will notice."

Is she out of her mind? Zach Bentley spends every waking hour playing Dungeons & Dragons down in his basement with his demented friends. That is, when he's not shoving kids into lockers and farting on them. He wouldn't notice her if she fell out of a tree onto his head.

The girls kept talking about how adorable Zach was, but they all clammed up when the bedroom door suddenly opened. A blond woman came in.

Wait, I recognized her! It was Carrie, the girl who keeps popping up and saving my life or having me save hers. Except now she looked old enough to be my *mom*!

"Carrie!" I exclaimed.

"Huh?" Everybody looked at me as if I was nuts.

"I need to . . . carry . . . my Barbie dolls up to the attic," I said weakly, "because I don't play with them anymore."

"Mom," Sue said, "I wish you would knock before barging into my room."

"Sorry, sweetie!" Sue's mother said. "Oh hi, Jennifer. I didn't see you come in."

"It's almost like I materialized out of thin air," I explained.

"Did you girls finish your homework?" Sue's mom asked.

"Yes, Mrs. McCormick," they all replied robotically.

"We started it the minute we got home from school," Sue told her.

What is their problem? Don't they know you're not supposed to start your homework until a few minutes before bedtime?

"Good," Sue's mom said. "I'll see you girls later. I love you."

"I love you too, Mom."

Sue's mom closed the door.

"My mom is such a pain," Sue said. "I wish I was an orphan."

"Me too," agreed Midori. "All my parents ever do is criticize me."

"I'm hungry," said Sharon, as if that had anything to do with what they were talking about.

I was hungry too. I wish I had some of those chips and pretzels I volunteered to bring. I thought the girls were going to go get some food, but they just sat there as if nobody had said anything about being hungry.

"What do you want to do?" asked Maria.

"I don't know. What do *you* want to do?" asked Midori.

"Let's talk about everything we did today," suggested Sue. "Then, let's talk about all the things we're going to do tomorrow!"

"That's a great idea!" said Sharon.

And that's exactly what they did, for like a half an hour. They talked about every class they were in, every teacher who said anything to them, every boy who looked at them, every girl who complimented their clothes, and every person who snubbed them. They talked about who was mean, who they weren't going to invite to their birthday parties, who had a crush on who, who they were going to sit next to at lunch the next day, and everything they ate.

I had never seen anybody talk so much and so fast. They kept interrupting each other and changing subjects. I wouldn't have been able to get a word in edgewise if I had tried. It was amazing. I always wondered what girls did after school.

"You've been really quiet, Jenn," Maria said, looking all concerned. "What did *you* do today?"

I didn't know what to say. I couldn't tell them I was pushed out of a plane and saw an alien and went to the moon and found the Magical Gold-Plated Knick-Knack.

"I . . . don't remember," I lied.

"Jennifer must be in *love!*" Sharon said, giggling.

"No *wonder* you've been so quiet!" said Maria.

"Jennifer, who do you have a crush on?" asked Midori.

"Nobody."

"Oh, come on, you *must* have a crush on *some-body!*" Sue said.

"You can tell us," Sharon said. "Remember, Friends 4 Life?"

"Jenn has a *secret* crush!" Midori said.

"Who's your secret crush, Jenn?" demanded Sue.

"Let's tell secrets!" Maria said, all excited. "Jennifer, you go first."

Well, at least they weren't asking me to say who I had a crush on anymore. I tried to think of a secret to tell them.

"Uh . . . one time I used the boys' bathroom at school," I said.

"Big deal," Sue said. "So did I."

"Me too," said Sharon.

"So did I," said Maria.

"Uh . . . ," I said, trying to come up with a better one. "One time at camp, somebody dared me to eat a worm. So I did."

"Ewwwwww!" they all went. "That's disgusting!"

"Hey, I have an idea," said Sue. "Let's bake something!"

"Yeah!" they all agreed.

These girls are crazy. When you're hungry, you don't bake something. You *eat* something. Baking takes time and effort. If you're hungry, you should eat something that somebody *else* baked.

They went into a long discussion about what they should bake. Sue wanted to bake cookies. Sharon wanted to bake cupcakes. Midori wanted to bake muffins. In the time they spent arguing over what they were going to bake, they could have baked something and eaten it already.

I was starting to get sleepy. It had been such a long day and these girls were so boring, I was afraid I was going to just fall asleep right there in the bean-bag chair.

"I have an idea," Sue said. "How about we make funnel cakes?"

Huh?!

Suddenly, I wasn't sleepy anymore. Did I hear that right? Did she say funnel cake, the most fantastic thing to eat in the world? Nobody bakes a funnel cake. You buy them on the boardwalk or at a carnival. I must not have heard her correctly.

"Uh, what was that you said?" I asked.

"I said let's bake a funnel cake!" Sue gushed.

"I think that's a *great* idea!" I exclaimed.

Everyone else thought so too, so we scampered downstairs and into the kitchen. I had to be careful not to trip in my pink sneakers.

Sue's mother even had a recipe for funnel cake

and a special pitcher with a funnel at the bottom that you use to make it. Huh! I didn't know they used a funnel. I thought it was called a funnel cake because some guy named Funnel invented it.

Ingredients for Funnel Cake

4 large eggs

1 tablespoon sugar

1 cup milk

6 tablespoons butter

1 cup flour

1/8 teaspoon salt

2 teaspoons baking powder

Vegetable oil

Powdered sugar

Wait a minute! I can't believe I'm actually writing out a recipe!

Sue gathered all the ingredients on the counter. Maria cracked the eggs into a bowl and beat them. Then Sharon added sugar, milk, flour, salt, butter and baking powder. Midori added more flour until the batter was smooth. It smelled delicious, and we hadn't even cooked it yet.

Sue took out a big pan, put it on the stove, and got a flame going under it. I poured some vegetable oil into the pan. Sharon poured the batter into the special pitcher that had the funnel thing on it. She held her finger on the bottom so the batter wouldn't drain out yet. Then Sue held the pitcher over the pan and Sharon took her finger off. The batter started dripping out of the bottom. It sizzled as soon as it hit the oil. Sue moved the pitcher over the pan, criss-crossing back and forth to make a big circular pattern, sort of like the head of a tennis racquet.

After a minute or so, Midori picked up the funnel cake with a pair of tongs to check it. When it was golden brown on the bottom, she flipped it over and let it fry for about a minute on the other side. Then Midori pulled it out of the pan with the tongs and let the extra oil drip onto a paper towel.

The whole time we were working on the funnel cake, the girls talked about how much they weigh, how fattening funnel cakes are, who was skinnier, what size clothes they wore, which stores they shopped at, and how they were not going to eat funnel cake for a year after they finished eating this one.

Finally, Sharon sprinkled powdered sugar on top of the funnel cake. My mouth was watering. It was worth it to be a girl for a while, I decided, if I could eat funnel cake as part of the deal. Sue passed out plates for all of us. I could almost taste the funnel cake.

"I'll get napkins for everybody," Sue said.

Napkins? I had heard of such things, but I had never actually touched one before. Sue handed me a napkin. It felt sort of papery.

I wanted to just grab a piece of that delicious funnel cake and stuff it into my mouth with both hands, but everybody else was being neat and waiting her turn. It was okay. I had waited a long time to have my first piece of homemade funnel cake. I could wait a minute longer.

"Do you want a big piece or a little piece, Jenn?" Sue asked me.

"Oh, I'd better have a little one," I heard myself saying. "I don't want to put on too much weight."

"You can always have another piece later," she said.

Sue put a piece on my plate. The smell of it was overwhelming. This is what it smells like in heaven all day long, I decided. I would bet that in heaven, even the bathrooms smell like funnel cake.

I picked it up.

I closed my eyes.

I put it into my mouth.

Chapter 12
Awakening

I put it into my mouth.

Ugh! It tasted bad. That had to be the worst funnel cake ever! It tasted like paper.

"Oh man, check it out," I heard somebody say. "Dinkleman is chewing on a *book*!"

I opened my eyes to see a bunch of people gathered around, staring at me. Lionel was there and a bunch of other kids and teachers.

"Are you okay, Trip?" asked our media specialist, Miss Durkin.

"Huh? What?" I said groggily. "Where's the funnel cake?"

"Funnel cake?" Miss Durkin said, laughing. "Trip, that's a *book* you're eating!"

She was right! I removed the book from my mouth and looked around. There were books scattered on the floor around me. Horror books and sports books, and fantasies and mysteries and adventure stories. I was sitting on the floor of the media center, behind one of the book-fair crates.

"You've been in this corner for *hours*, Trip," Miss Durkin told me. "It's time to close up the book fair, but I didn't want to disturb you. You were just so immersed in all these books that you must have lost track of the time."

"I missed lacrosse tryouts!" I shouted. "Now I won't make the team!"

"It's pouring out, Dink," Lionel said. "That's why we're all in here. They rescheduled the tryouts for tomorrow."

The door opened and the school nurse, Mrs. Robinson, came in, with Principal Miller.

"Hello there! Anybody home?" Principal Miller said. "I just dropped by because I heard the boy— well, he seems all right now."

"You're *alive*?" I asked him.

"Of course I'm alive!" Principal Miller replied.

"Trip got quite a bump on the head," Mrs. Robinson told Principal Miller. "We kind of thought for a moment he was going to leave us."

"I *did* leave you, Mrs. Robinson!" I told her. "I was in a haunted house, and I saw an alien in Washington! I was on a quest for a gold-plated knick-knack! I was even trapped in a dictionary! And all of you were accused of murdering Principal Miller!"

"There, there," she said, putting a hand on my forehead. "Lie quietly now."

A bunch of other people came over.

"Remember me, your old pal Mrs. Babcock?"

"And me, Mrs. Pontoon of the PTA?"

"You couldn't forget my face, could you?" said the custodian, Mr. Dunn.

Ahh! He looked just like Professor Psycho!

"It wasn't just books," I said. "It felt like I was *at* all these places. And you, and you, and you, and you were there. But you couldn't have been, could you?"

"We imagine lots of things when we read a good book," Miss Durkin said.

"I remember that some of it wasn't very nice," I told them. "Like when that guy tried to steal my face and when I was a cat. But most of it was awesome, like when I was in the Super Bowl and walking on the moon. Just the same, all I kept saying to everybody was I want to go home. And they sent me home!"

All the grown-ups chuckled.

"Doesn't anybody believe me?" I asked.

"Of course we believe you, Trip," Miss Durkin said.

"But anyway I'm home," I said, "and this is my school and you're all here, and I'm not going to leave here ever again."